K.E. MONTEITH

A BROTHER'S BEST FRIEND ROMANCE

ALL GROWN UP

K.E. Monteith

For Monica, who listened to me ramble on about this book since its inception.

CONTENTS

CONTENT WARNINGS

Please note this book contains sexually explicit scenes that may be inappropriate for younger audiences.

CHAPTER 1

Kaleb

I have been in love with Lexi Jacobs for my whole life.

Well, most of my life. And love might be a stretch because the last time we saw each other I was still a gangly teen in the throes of adolescence, unable to hold a full conversation with any girl, let alone my big brother's best friend. And Blake, fully aware of my "crush" since he found a picture of Lexi at the beach, the half where he would have stood ripped off, under my pillow, would always make a point of mentioning just how cute and little I was in Lexi's presence. Which of course led to me being flustered and leaving the room.

But I wasn't 14 and inexperienced anymore. I wasn't going to freeze up or stutter my words or run away because I'd pitched a tent from the way she leaned over me to grab something and her breast grazed my chest. Bottom line, I wasn't going to embarrass myself, I was going to be a man. And I was going to get her to notice me and, if I was lucky, fall for me too.

"Kaleb! Lexi's here, can you help get her things?" Mom shouted from the front door.

Fuck, I was not prepared for this. Blake and his fiancé were staying at a hotel as they finished up wedding preparations/party all week long and Lexi, whose family had since moved, was going to stay in Blake's old room for the week. Which meant we'd be sleeping on the other side of the wall from each other and sharing a bathroom. It was like my best dream and worst nightmare mixed into one.

"Coming!" I shouted back to Mom, though my feet hadn't moved. Instead of leaving my bedroom, I stood in front of the mirror on my dresser, trying to tamp down my mess of brown curls. Damn, I should've gotten a haircut before I left. But it was too late to do anything about it now, if I brushed it, it would just be a frizzy mess.

I rushed out of my room and down the stairs, taking two steps at a time. And there she was, Lexi Jacobs, standing in my living room and hugging my mom like they would never let go of each other. Mom always did treat Lexi like the daughter she never had. And even if she didn't say it out loud, I could tell she was disappointed Lexi and Blake never got together. Even my mom didn't consider me a viable dating option for Lexi and that was a little more than vexing.

But that would change this week. I wasn't incompetent anymore, I had experience with women, I could make Lexi see me for me. Not a kid or somebody's little brother. A man. A man who would do absolutely anything for her.

"Hey, Lex," I said after clearing my throat. The women broke their hug and Lexi's hazel eyes brightened when she looked up at me. And god damn, her Instagram photos had *not* done her justice. After not seeing her in person in 10 years, you'd think she'd be strikingly different, but she wasn't, not really. All the things I loved about Lexi stayed the same. She still had the soft, almost imperceivable freckles over her nose, still had eyes that reminded me of fall, and still dressed like she just came from a pickup game. But the small changes, the womanly changes, moved my sweet tender feelings to something a little hotter.

"Kiddie Kay, look at you! You're a whole head taller than me now." Lexi crossed over to me and wrapped her arms around my waist. I had to fight so many emotions at once, my body wasn't sure what to do. That dumb nickname made me want to groan and point out that my height proved I was no longer a kid. But the way her breasts were pushed together in her purple-ish sports bra distracted me and then it was too late to complain about her calling me a kid. A kid sure as hell wouldn't have been enjoying the view like I was doing. But a man would've been able to control his urges to look. Fuck, I've gotta get my head back on straight.

"Well, it has been a while. How're you doing?" I asked once she let go with two small pats on my back. And damn, I hope my voice didn't sound as strained as it felt.

"It really has been too long. I don't think I've been back since my parents moved and that was, what? Ten years ago. Geez. But I've been good. I'm excited for the wedding. It's gonna be just like old times, right?"

Before I had a chance to reply, Mom started meandering towards the kitchen, shouting when we were still just a few feet away, "Can I get you guys anything to drink? Dinner should be ready in ten, Blake and Kat should be here around then too."

"Oh thanks, can I get some of your sweet tea? They don't make it like you do up north. If I order some, they always bring me unsweetened and sugar packets. It's just not the same, you know?" Lexi said, smiling in my mother's direction even though she was blocked from view. In the kitchen, Mom tsk-ed loudly and started pulling out cups.

"I'll take a beer, Mom." Then turning to Lexi, whose eyes were starting to widen, "Your things still in the car?"

"Um, yeah, but I can get them later." She sounded flustered, her hands waving around. I raised a brow at her but, because I was trying to look cool, just walked outside to her car and tried to keep from smiling when I heard her follow behind me.

"So you drink now?" Lexi asked from behind me.

"Sure, why wouldn't I? I'm 24, seems to be a pretty reasonable drinking age."

"I guess I just expected you to be the same kid from before," she mumbled. I stopped at her trunk, opened it up, and looked at her over her shoulders. My eyes glazed down her body, the way I'd done with other girls before, but the second I looked back to her eyes, I looked away. I wasn't *just* attracted to Lexi. And we weren't in some bar or club. I shouldn't be giving her that look here and now.

"Well, I've grown up some these last few years," I mumbled, pulling out her bags and one of those clothes hanger bags, which folded over my arm in a familiar way that a dress shouldn't.

"You're training to become a physical therapist, right?"

"Yeah, I graduate in a couple of months. Can I take a peek?" I held up the clothing bag and she nodded, her head tilted as if she had no clue why I would want to look. Of course she wouldn't know that I was torn between wanting to see her in something low cut and something that wouldn't draw any other guys' attention. But apparently, I had no reason to worry, because it was a suit.

"Why do you have a tux?"

"Cause I'm the best man."

My jaw dropped and so did the tux.

"That mother fucker."

"Wait, did Blake not tell you?" Lexi stepped up, reaching for the clothes at the same time I did. Our fingers grazed and I froze for a second too long and she picked up the bag.

"He told me you were a part of the wedding party. So I just assumed you were a bridesmaid. Kat was your roommate back at Penn, right?"

"She was, that's how they met. They flipped a coin to see whose side I'd stand on and Blake won. To be honest, I'm relieved he did. Nothing against Kat, I love her to death, but Blake's been my ride or die since we were kids, you know? Plus tuxedos have pockets and I won't feel pressured to wear heels." We started back to the house and I tried not to look at the way she clutched the bag to her chest and the effect it had on my body.

"I know." A fear that had struck me since childhood, that she and Blake had ever been a thing, returned and I tried to get a read on if she was sad that she wasn't the one marrying Brad. But if she was, she was hiding it really well. Maybe it was just me projecting my insecurities on her.

We didn't say anything else as we walked up the stairs and to Blake's room, but the instant she stepped inside, she lit up again.

"Oh my god, it hasn't changed a bit!"

"Nah, Mom likes to keep our rooms as little time capsules for when we're gone. All our little league trophies and science fair ribbons are right where we left them. Though I'm pretty sure she threw out Blake's porn stash." I set her things down on Blake's bed and wiped my hands together, trying not to cringe at bringing up porn. "Drinks?"

"Oh yeah. Um, I kinda wanna unpack and, you know, dig up some dirt on Blake for my speech."

And I wanted to sit and just watch her, but that sounded creepy, so I left her to it.

CHAPTER 2

Lexi

Shit, Kaleb Russel grew up to be a smoke show. Damn. I mean, I'd seen his gym pics on Instagram, so I knew, but I didn't really know. He wasn't big and bulky, just very well toned. And shit, I should not have been looking at my best friend's little brother like that. At least he didn't catch me checking him out, or at least I hope he didn't because I was probably drooling as he walked in front of me to the car. The man, because he was a man now, had a nice ass.

I took a deep breath in. And then another and convinced myself it was out of my system. Kaleb wasn't a kid anymore, that was for damn sure, but being physically attracted to him just meant I wasn't blind, nothing more.

Distracting myself, I started unpacking my things and hung my suit in the almost empty closet. Remembering what Kay had said, I reached around the closet wall where Blake had taped an oversized ziplock bag filled with porn mags and a USB drive. When we were teenagers Blake showed me his porn stash, claiming that I needed to watch it so that I knew what other guys would expect. But of course he immediately popped a boner and I threw a basketball at him. That was what happened any time we toed that line of intimacy because everyone was convinced we were meant to be together. Even Kat was for a while. But that attraction just wasn't there. Even when he got that boner, he immediately assured me it was for the actress and not me. Which, phew.

But Kay was right, the stash was gone. So much for that best man story fodder. Though I guess I could tell the story without the evidence. If I was being honest, this best man's speech was stressing me out. I have one more week to come up with something perfect and hilarious, appropriate for friends and family, and I had absolutely nothing. And this week was filled up with wedding event after wedding event. I think the only free day was the day before the wedding. Maybe Kaleb could help me write it? Between the two of us, we knew Blake's whole life story.

I changed out of my comfy driving clothes and into jeans and a turtleneck. Partly because it was edging on fall, the tree with a fort outside Blake's window already changing colors, and partly because of that look Kaleb gave me outside, like he was checking me out. When we were kids, he was always awkward with me, but what kid wasn't awkward around the sex they liked? This look was different though. It was practiced. Like he knew how to look a girl up and down to make her shiver. And I didn't exactly like the idea that the sweet kid I knew had turned into a player.

I looked into Blake's closet mirror, trying to see what Kay was looking at. And I'm not one to overestimate myself, but I did have some nice ass curves. So yeah, Kaleb was just doing what I'd done. Appreciating the changes in our bodies and recognizing that we were two attractive individuals. It's not like he was making a move or anything, so it meant nothing. Absolutely nothing.

The second I stepped out of Blake's room, a cacophony of voices rose from downstairs and I rushed down to my best friends' voices. At the base of the stairs, Blake and Kat were taking turns hugging the other members of the Russel family. Without a second's hesitation, I jumped in to join Kay hugging Blake. I thought I heard somebody gulp, but between the two tall guys and Kat talking with their parents, I wasn't sure where it came from or if I was just hearing things.

"Lex!" Blake said, letting go of his brother and wrapping his arms around me and picking me up just a foot before setting me down. "I haven't seen you in, like, three weeks!"

"I know, how have you managed?" I asked, laughing. And was that a frown on Kaleb's face? Did he think I was monopolizing his brother? Shit, that would make sense. Blake, Kat, and I all live in Philadelphia together, barely a 15-minute walk apart, we see each other all the time. Kaleb probably only sees his brother on holidays now. Note to self, let the brothers have some brotherly bonding time.

"Well, Kat's pretty good company," he said with a shrug, making Kat stop midconversation to playfully slap his arm. "But how was the drive? My room to your liking?"

"Drive was meh. I was listening to that one crime/ghost podcast you were telling me about and I think you should definitely stop listening to it before bed, that can't be healthy."

"I told you," Kat said, crossing over to me for a hug before hugging Kaleb. I eyed the two, curious to see how they got along. But there was no awkwardness with their hug, no awkward patting like I'd done, and Kay's smile seemed genuine. That was a relief. Kat had talked about Kaleb and said they'd gotten along, but an anxious part of me couldn't believe it until I saw it. The Russell's have been like family since I was little and Kat was like a sister to me. I would've been crushed if they didn't get along.

"And your room's fine. Though your porn stash has been cleared out."

"Mom," Blake cried, just as his mother said, "Lexi! Why on Earth were you looking for that?"

"Best man's speech fodder." His mom rolled her eyes at that and their dad laughed as he left for the dining room. He'd never been a man of many words. He seemed to like to sit in the room and watch his boys grow without interfering much.

"Well no more porn talk, please. Dinner's ready."

We all shuffled to the dining room. Before taking his seat, Blake grabbed Kaleb into a headlock, ruffling up his little brother's hair. One glance at Kaleb's bit lip and the way he had to lean down for his brother to reach, I could tell that Kaleb was letting his brother do this and if he wanted, he could flip Blake over easily. And that … was not something I needed to think about and was none of my business. I'm sure Kaleb had a girlfriend or something from school and she wouldn't appreciate me thinking about him flipping me on his bed. Shit, I shouldn't have even finished that thought.

"Can you believe how big Kiddie Kay's gotten, Lex? He's taller than me now, the bastard."

"Your brother isn't a bastard," their father assured from the table without looking up from his paper. The boys pushed off each other and took their seats at the table. I used to sit beside Blake, across from Kay. But with Kat taking that spot, which was rightfully her's, I settled in next to Kaleb.

The table had already been set with each of our plates full of fried chicken, mashed potatoes, and peas, with extra servings and rolls set in the middle. Once everyone was seated, we all dug in without ceremony. Because that's how things were at the Russel home, food first, conversation second.

"Kay, what made you decide to go into PT?" I asked, once we'd started to slow our eating and conversation wouldn't be had through full mouths.

"I had to do PT in high school and thought it was cool," he answered with a shrug.

"But also because he's half muscle head and he thinks being a personal trainer is lame," Blake said with a mischievous smile. Kaleb rolled his eyes but didn't look up to Blake. And since Blake didn't get the rise he wanted, he added, "And because he had the hots for his therapist."

Kaleb looked up from his food to his brother, eyes narrowed, but didn't say anything. And their mother interjected with, "No, she wasn't his therapist. You're thinking of his doctor. She was beautiful. But too old for you, Kay, dear."

"I didn't have a crush on any of the *professionals* who helped me with my torn tendon," Kaleb grumbled, looking back to his food to avoid Blake's grin. I knew that grin. That was the, let's-see-how-far-we-can-push-this grin. The drinking-all-night-before-exams-will-be-fine grin. The I-don't-mind-getting-in-a-bit-of-trouble grin. I knew it well.

"You're right, you were probably still hung up over --" And instead of finishing that sentence, Blake was hit square in the mouth with a roll.

"Kaleb, no throwing food. You'd think you'd have grown out of that," their mother grumbled.

"No worries, Ma. I deserved it. Plus if he really wanted to be a prick about it, he would've flung potatoes at me." Blake picked up the roll that'd fallen to his plate and took a big bite, keeping eye contact with his brother, who shrugged innocently.

"Don't know what you're talking about."

"Sure, sure. Don't worry Kiddie Kay, I won't spill the beans. Ow, babe." The last few words were after a loud thud underneath the table.

"You deserve it. Stop being a dick to your brother, " Kat said, huffing and flipping her hair at Blake.

"Finally a sibling I can get along with, I'm taking Kat's side in the eventual divorce," Kaleb said, exchanging bright smiles with Kat. And just like that, the conversation was dropped. And it seemed like I was the only one who didn't understand what they were talking about. And I wasn't used to being out of the loop in the Russel house.

CHAPTER 3

Kaleb

I stared at the ceiling of my room listening for signs of life coming from Blake's old room. I didn't hear anything, so either Lexi was still asleep some 10 feet away from me, or she'd already gotten up.

God, she looked so confused at dinner last night. Which I should be grateful for, but that sad look in her eyes afterward, like we'd left her out of some inside joke, killed me. I wanted to wrap my arm around her shoulder, kiss her forehead, and reassure her she was still a part of this family and always had been. But even if I reassured her in a less romantic way, I don't think she'd take comfort from me. Not when she was still thinking of me as *Kiddie Kay*. God, I wanted to punch Blake so bad every time he called me that, give him a nice shiner for his wedding day. But I couldn't do that to Kat. That woman is *way* too good for him. And she saved my ass last night too. My only plan to combat Blake's jackassness was to not respond, but one word from her shut him down. God bless.

Climbing out of bed, I meandered out to the hall, checking that Blake's door was closed before heading into the bathroom.

"Oh, shit, fuck, sorry," I murmured, because I opened the bathroom door without checking to see if a light was on and walked right into Lexi in a towel, hair wet and droplets of water still clinging to her skin. I immediately averted my eyes and closed the door on the tempting scene.

"It's all right, I'm fully covered. I guess I should've locked the door. You're not used to having to check if anyone's here, right?" she said from inside the bathroom. The door creaked open and her head popped out. "I'm just fixing up my hair. So you can come in if you need to grab something or brush your teeth or whatever."

"Oh, yeah, I just need to brush my teeth," I lie, raking my fingers through my hair, praying she doesn't notice the start of my body reacting to her in a towel. She smiled and opened the door all the way, walking back to the counter top where she had several products lined up. So much for the effortless tomboy image I had of her.

But I wanted to show her I was a man, this was as good a chance as any. I had just wandered out of my room in my boxers, so she got a full show.

I walked in and over to the sink, passing behind Lexi and getting a big whiff of her soap. Apples and cinnamon.

"Do you mind if I close the door? I wanna keep in

the warm air."

"Sure." I'm pretty sure I choked out the word, but Lexi didn't seem to notice as she closes the door, shutting us in together.

I distract myself from the lump in my throat by brushing my teeth, keeping my eyes on my own reflection in the mirror.

My eyes flashed over to her, curious to see if my lack of clothes had any effect on her. What did she think? Was she the type who saw any kind of definition as trying too hard? I tried to side-eye her, but she was too busy futzing with her hair to look at me. She seemed completely unperturbed by my presence and it kind of hurt. It's not like I wanted her fawning all over me, just to … be aware, look at me and get a little flushed.

"Do you do this a lot?"

"Do what?" She finally stopped messing with her hair to look at me, her gaze fluttering over my chest for just a second before focusing on my eyes. Good. She's at least aware I have a body. That's a great first step.

"Hang out in a towel with some half-naked guy," I say before spitting out the toothpaste and grabbing the mouthwash. I turned back to look at Lexi and her cheeks had reddened, hazel eyes gone wide.

"Of course not! It's just you, you know. I can trust you … right?" she stumbled through the words, turning away from me almost immediately and bending over so her hair fell toward the floor. She gathered up her hair into a ponytail, reaching up awkwardly to grab a tie from the counter. And as her hand stretched, the towel started slipping down her back. Instinctively, I dropped the mouthwash and took the step over her to hold the towel up and keep her covered.

"Sorry, I didn't mean you couldn't trust me. I was just a little worried. I'll always have your back, Lex," I said, averting my eyes as Lexi readjusted and tied the towel back in place.

"Um, thanks, I -- sorry, thanks, Kaleb." She didn't turn back to face me, just went straight out of the bathroom. But I could still see the nape of her neck and the tips of her ears redden.

I could take that as progress, right?

But before I had a chance to dwell on that possible progress, I locked the bathroom door, hopped into a cold, cold shower, and tried not to dwell on how the towel rose over her ass as she walked away or how her scent still lingered in the shower.

❋ ❋ ❋

I jogged down stairs, staring at an obnoxious text from Blake reminding me about his party tonight and how I should be Lexi's DD. As if I wasn't already planning on it. When I looked up, Lexi was sitting on the couch in tight jeans and a low cut shirt, her hair braided to one side and a dark pink-ish color painting her lips. I don't think I've ever seen her dressed up like this. It was casual but still put together. It was the kind of look you wore to a bar if you didn't mind getting hit on, not too eye-catching to purposely draw attention, but just enough to catch somebody's eye if they were already looking.

"Ready?" I ask, clearing my throat to draw her attention away from her phone. When she looked at me, she bit her lip and looked away, nodding and hopping off the couch. I followed behind her, grabbing her hand when she reached for her keys.

"I'm DD. We'll take my car."

"Oh you don't have to do that," she said, pulling her hand away from mine quickly. Ouch.

"Yeah I do. This event's a bunch of friends from college and high school, right? You should have fun, drink as much as you want. I'll make sure you get back here safely. Unless you were planning on ..." I let my voice trail off, wincing at the idea of her going back to some dude's hotel. I chanced a look at Lexi, her head tilted, nose scrunched. And damn, that confused look flooded me with relief. "Nothing, sorry. I'm driving, end of story."

I grabbed my keys, walking out the door with her and locking up behind us.

"Oh." I turned to Lexi, her face reddening again as she caught on to my unspoken question. I wasn't trying to make her blush this much. Was that a good thing?

"No, I'm not planning on going ... on that. Of that pool of people, I've already tried it with anyone I was interested in and I highly doubt your brother would have invited those guys. This one guy we went to college with sorta cheated on me, we hadn't really been exclusive or even dating that long, but Blake punched him. And got us banned from that club. So it's safe to say none of my exes will be there."

None of that was what I wanted to hear. But I mentally gave Blake a clap on the back. He was a dick to me most of the time, but he did take care of Lexi and I could respect that.

"I would've done the same." I opened up the passenger side door of my car for her, watching as she settled in, giving me an unreadable look before smiling.

"Kay, if you punched him, he would've ended up concussed. Seriously, how much time do you spend at the gym?"

Ah, it felt good hearing her complement my body. Even if it was indirect. I gave her a smile, one that I hoped wasn't as eager as I felt, and closed her door. Once I was settled in the driver's seat, I felt her eyes grazing over my body with a question. And I was more than willing to answer anything she asked of me and more.

"My injury wasn't anything crazy or life-changing, but I wasn't able to move on my own for so long that my whole left side lost muscles. From my hip down, everything felt uneven. PT helped with most of that, but that sensation drove me crazy, so I, you know, went the extra step to make things feel normal."

"How'd you injure yourself? If you don't mind me asking."

"You can ask me anything, Lex." I let my words

hang there for a moment, running my tongue over my lip and resisting taking my eyes off the road to look at her. "It's not some crazy story. Just twisted my ankle at a very unnatural angle during a game."

"Soccer, right?"

"Yeah, we were sort of pummeling the other team, so the coach put in the newbies. And they kinda took offense to that and upped their game. The guy who pushed me got a red card, so, you know, there's that, I guess."

"Can you still play?"

"Eh, I could, but it'd be risky. The doctor pretty much said, if I took one more hit like that, I'd be donezo. So Mom, of course, didn't want me to play again and Dad was just, your body, your choice."

"Nice," Lexi cut in, making us both laugh.

"But after all the work I had to do in PT and all the extra shit I did on my own, I just sorta didn't feel like it was worth the risk. I mean, I hadn't really been a star player or anything. It's not like I was on the verge of joining the MLS. So it didn't feel like I was losing much."

"You could've though. I mean, I only went to a couple of your games in middle school. And I don't know much about soccer. But I thought you were a star player."

This was what I loved about Lexi. She built people up. And when I say people, I mean everybody. She saw someone playing on the streets of D.C., she stopped and complemented their style or how they played. And if you were her friend, she told you exactly what you needed to hear to lift your spirits. Even if you were just her friend's kid brother who just lost his first middle school soccer game.

"Thanks, Lex. That means a lot. But I'm okay, really. And hey, the incident helped me figure out what I wanna do with my life. That's pretty cool. I can help some kid who was in my shoes and maybe get him fixed up even better so he doesn't have to weigh the risks of playing again."

"When'd you get so cool, Kiddie Kay?"

Damn that nickname.

"Somewhere between when you left and now."

"I guess so."

CHAPTER 4

Lexi

The Purple Fish hadn't changed a bit since I was last here. The pub wasn't exactly a dive, but it was shabby and covered in wood, floor to ceiling. And years after the rise of hipsters, they somehow still managed to pack every corner. Except for the back row of tables where the wedding crowd was gathered under an "Almost Married" banner.

As soon as we approached, I was sucked into conversations with old high school friends. But I didn't miss how Kaleb hung to the edge of the crowd. Or how the second I left his side some of the hipster girls approached him. I rolled my eyes at the sight of the cropped topped, flannel with leggings girls, twirling their hair at Kaleb. These girls weren't his type. Though I didn't actually know that, did I? And he sure was smiling nicely at them, the little dimples in his cheek showing. And he leaned in when they spoke to him.

Nope. That was none of my business. There's

probably a reason Kaleb's never talked to me about his dating life. It'd be like telling your big sister, right?

I focused back on my friends and their stories about their wonderful partners and babies. And I was so focused on being focused and not thinking about Kaleb or being single, that I jumped when something brushed against my shoulder.

"Oh sorry, just thought you needed a drink," Kaleb said, holding a glass of root beer in one hand and a fruity looking drink in the other. He set the drink in my hand and just as I was about to ask how he knew what I drank, Jason, one of Blake's high school buddies who I didn't really care for, wrapped his arm around Kaleb's neck.

"Kiddie Kay! How ya doing, man? Whatcha drinking?" Jason asked, already slurring his words. Kaleb winced at the nickname, but quickly covered it with a polite smile. I instantly felt guilty calling him that just a few minutes ago. Of course he wouldn't want to be called a kid, he was a full grown man. A well endowed man given what I saw from his boxers this morning. But it was so hard to stop calling him a name we'd been using for years.

"I'm good, Jay. And I've just got a root beer. Apparently it's locally grown or some shit. The girl at the bar gave me some big spiel about it, but it was hard to hear over the crowd." Kaleb squinted at the label as if all the information the bartender told him would be listed there. I took a glance at the bar to find a petite blonde eyeing Kaleb. Yeah, she definitely was angling for more than a good tip. And what was with my sudden urge to put a hand on Kay? To say that she wasn't good enough for him?

"Ah, does Blake have you playing DD for Lex?" Jay asked and Kaleb nodded. And that made me ... disappointed? Why? Of course Blake made sure I had someone drive me home and Kaleb was the most logical choice. But he deserved to have fun and drink too, because he was apparently a casual drinker now. And I guess I wanted him to want to be my DD and not just do it because Blake told him to.

Nope, I was thinking about this too much. It was time to drink.

* * *

Pleasantly buzzed and seated between Kaleb and Blake, no, Blake and Kaleb, we started sharing stories about our high school days, alternating between Kat's friends ratting her out for the footballer she had a crush on and Blake's crew telling the story about how one of Jason's parties got busted up by the cops.

"And it happened again like five years later with my lil brother. Same cop and everything. Right, Kay?" Jason said, pointing his cup to Kaleb, splashing his beer on the table.

"I didn't stick around long enough to find out."

"That's my lil bro!" Blake cheered, leaning around me to clasp Kay on the shoulder. I liked it when they got along. Even if Blake was just congratulating Kaleb for not getting caught for drinking underage. I was an only child, so seeing them act the part of a happy family really hit me.

"Oh, that's right, you left with that one smoke show. Um ... what was her name? She was a cheerleader, right?" Jay asked, tapping his glass against his head. I chanced a glance at Kaleb to see him blushing ever so slightly.

"Her name was Angela, and she was a tennis player, not a cheerleader."

"Ah whatever, she was hot." Jay leaned over to the guy next to him and said, "Don't let your innocent memories fool you. I went to undergrad with him and he's got game."

"Jay." Kaleb's voice was more warning than anything else. I squinted at him, trying to figure out how the kid I knew became this man, who apparently had women crawling all over him. I guess I couldn't blame them, my body sure as hell had a reaction to him.

"What? That whole injured player thing put you in a sweet spot in high school. And by the time you got to college, you really hit your stride."

"Jay."

"Shut up, Jay! We're supposed to be talking about me," Blake chimed in, shooting a grumpy scowl at Jason.

"Well, Lexi has all your dirt." Everyone turned to me with expectant eyes, except for Kaleb, who was focused on the remnants of his root beer.

"Um, have I already told the story of our first kiss?" The crowd cheered for me to go on, while Blake and Kat groaned in mock disgust. Beside me, I thought I felt Kaleb go still. But I must've been imagining things from all the drinks. Surely he'd heard this story before.

"So we we're, what? Thirteen, you know, the age where you start getting curious about what kissing is like. And this dumbass here tells me that we might as well try it out. Cause it's not like we'd be embarrassed or nervous to kiss each other, so we could get … I dunno, used to it before we found someone we wanted to kiss."

"No, no, no, you were the one that told me that," Blake interjected.

"Agree to disagree. Anyways, we scurried up to his room, closed the door and sat on the bed. I think we spent, like, five minute just sitting there. Then we closed our eyes, put our lips together for like two seconds, and then immediately started gagging. His lips were somehow both chapped and damp. It's still the worst kiss I've ever had, to this day. And then the next day, we just wouldn't look at each other. I think we only started talking again because he fell out of the bus and I couldn't help but laugh at him. So all that to say, I'm sorry you're marrying such a shit kisser, Kat." I raised my drink to Kat, most everyone else doing the same and shouting their cheers. But beside me, Kaleb's glass came down with a loud thud and his chair squeaked back abruptly. By the time I looked over to him, he was already halfway to the back door that led to the bar's patio.

"That little twerp," Blake mumbled, getting up

and going after his brother.

"What's that about?" I asked, hoping into Blake's vacated seat to sit by Kat.

"Oh, just dumb, brother shit. You know," Kat said, waving her hand wildly, obviously a little drunk. But I didn't know what she was talking about. And I felt like I should.

"But Blake wasn't really messing with him. This time."

"Oh. … it's probably just some old fight. I wish Blake stopped picking on Kaleb, he's gonna get himself punched one day. Oh shit."

Without a word, I nodded and got up to head to where the brothers had gone, understanding Kat's worry. She might be cool if Kaleb gave Blake a black eye any other week, but not right before the wedding.

Just as I made it to the patio door, Blake came in, looking irritated but, thankfully, bruise-free.

"Oh good, Kat sent me to make sure there weren't any punches being thrown."

"What? Oh, yeah, no. Kaleb wouldn't hit me. He's too much of a punk for that. He just got his own feelings hurt. Just leave him be for now. If he leaves, I'll get you a cab."

"Oh, sure, thanks. But should I talk to him?" Blake shrugged, but didn't say anything, looking over his shoulder at the door. "Well, thanks for the drinks, anyways."

"What?"

"Oh, Kaleb brought me some drinks. I just assumed you had him bring them over."

"That little punk. What the hell does he think he's doing?" Blake looked back to the patio door again, ruffling his dark waves. Kaleb's hair had always been so much curlier, like their mom's. Had I always known that or was I just realizing it now? "Whatever. He bought you the drinks on his own, but don't worry about it. He's got this sweet internship slash assistant position at this PT office by his school. He's getting paid more than I did right after college. I think the boss is trying to bribe him to stay working there. So, you know, go ahead and rack up his tab."

Blake walked back to the table, greeted by loud cheers on his return. But instead of joining the party, I found myself heading out to the patio. Outside, Kaleb was leaning up against the wall, phone in hand. I stood next to him, rubbing my arms to stave off the cold of the incoming fall. Kaleb slid his phone into his pocket, took off his hoodie, and held it out for me.

"Oh thanks, but are you sure?" I took his still warm jacket, trying to resist the temptation of sliding my arms in as I waited for his response.

"I'm sure. You came out here to talk to me, right? Least I can do is keep you warm."

I pulled on the hoodie, ignoring the impulse to breathe in Kay's smell or think about how much bigger he was. The sweatshirt wasn't tight on him, but it didn't hide any of his definition. On me, it looked like I was wearing a bag. Beside me, Kaleb chuckled, like he was thinking the same thing.

"Don't laugh. I used to be bigger than you, Kiddie Kay." I wanted to take it back immediately when he winced.

"I'm not a kid anymore," he mumbled with a sigh.

"I know." I shifted in place, feeling my face warm up and hoping he'd attribute it to the alcohol and not realize I was thinking of him in his boxers this morning. Again.

Kaleb pushed off the wall and turned to me, leaning in with one hand resting against the wall by my face. Our bodies were mere inches apart and I could feel heat radiating off his body. But he hadn't been drinking, so why was he so hot? So fucking hot.

"You always saw me as a kid, didn't you?" Kaleb asked, his voice low, so low that the lower parts of my body stirred.

"I mean, you were a kid. So yeah, I did." I couldn't look him in the eye when he was this close and with the alcohol clouding my head, so my eyes settled on his full lips. And given the way he licked his lips, I figured he noticed. So I gulped and looked up to him properly.

"And now?" Kaleb pushed closer into me, my thighs up against his, and his head tilted beside mine, his voice tickling my ear. If I leaned into him, I knew I'd get a full feel of him. But I couldn't move, couldn't look away from his eyes. Because he wasn't my Kaleb. Not wholly. This Kaleb wasn't the one who stumbled with his words anytime we were alone together. This Kaleb knew how to be around women. And that was exactly my type, for better or worse. And it was almost always for the worse.

"Now I see you as a man." A glint in his eyes

broke me, made me fall into that temptation. Leaning against the wall, I pushed my hips into his, feeling the hard bulge in his pants, a groan vibrating against my ear. He pulled away with a jolt, eyes wide and throat bobbing.

"Sorry, you've had too much to drink. We should probably go and get you to bed. I mean, to sleep," he said after clearing his throat and taking a few steps away.

"Oh, okay." I moved to the door but stopped when Kaleb put a hand on my shoulder.

"Sorry. But the guys, well just Jason really, will give you crap if you go back in with my hoodie on. I don't want you to have to deal with that."

"Oh, okay," I repeated, not able to come up with any new words. But Kaleb was just like his brother, the way he kept me from unnecessary hassle. I guess it was a Russel thing.

Since I hadn't made a move to take the jacket off, Kaleb's fingers slid to my waist and under the hem. I felt him hesitantly touch the small of my back, the fabric of my shirt tucked in and secure so that when he slid the hoodie off me, nothing else came off. Except maybe I got off on it, a little, and the way he smoothed my hair back down from the static felt like a gesture intended to keep me from thinking of him taking off my clothes. But that was all I was thinking about. He'd had the opportunity to take a full gander this morning, why hadn't he? Was it because he wasn't interested? Did his heart not race when he took the hoodie off me?

"I'll meet you back at the car, okay?"

"Okay. Oh and thanks for the drinks," I added, wanting to say it before I forget and also wanting to prolong this heated moment, even if I couldn't bring myself to turn and face him. God, what would he think if he saw how red my face was? And how was I gonna face Blake knowing I practically felt up his brother?

"Of course. I'm a gentleman, I'm not gonna bring a girl out and not pay for her drinks."

"It's not like this is a date though." I laughed out the words and went to the door, hand on the knob.

"I know. But that doesn't stop me from wanting to treat you."

CHAPTER 5

Kaleb

Shit, fuck, shit, I'm such a dumbass dickbag. How could I hit on Lexi when she was drunk?

Because Blake had just called me out about getting upset about something that was 1) none of my business and 2) happened almost 15 years ago. And he was right, I shouldn't have gotten upset that Lexi's first kiss was with him, I had figured that was the case anyways. But damn, it still hurt to hear. Plus everyone kept calling me a kid and Jason was just running his mouth off about one of my exes. The kiss story was the last straw.

And then after Blake's lecture, there Lexi was, standing beside me shivering. And seeing her in my hoodie, damn. I let everything get to my head, impatient for a sign that she could at the very least see me and not the kid she remembered.

And I wasn't expecting her to press into me like that. Shit, if I'd been drinking too I would've kissed her then. Maybe more. Probably. No, definitely. I would've at the very least tried to dry hump her till she came. Thank god I was sober.

My car door opened and I pulled my head off the wheel to see Lexi settle into the passenger seat, her face still flushed. I shouldn't have bought her so many drinks, I'd forgotten how strong that fruit shit was and just ordered another one when she finished a cup. How many had it been? Four? Five? God, I hope she didn't think I was trying to get her drunk. Fuck. How did I always manage to screw things up with Lexi?

"Are you good, Lex? I didn't mean to get you so many drinks, I was just trying to, you know …" But I trailed off, not sure how to say that I wanted to make sure she was taken care of and having fun without implying anything.

"Oh I know, I didn't think you were … trying anything funny. You Russel boys take good care of your friends, I know that."

Yup, I was definitely just buying her drinks because we're friends. I always spent over $50 on my friends' drinks. Totally.

"Blake was telling me you had a job at some PT place and you were probably gonna stay there after you graduate." Lexi shifted in her seat, her thighs rubbing together. Nope, not looking. I'd done enough tonight.

"Yeah, they've already offered me a full-time job once I graduate. It's a pretty good gig. And Baltimore's a good distance between here and Blake, but I don't know. I'm not particularly interested in the city. The job would be convenient more than anything else."

"Is there anywhere you wanna live?"

With you.

"Not really."

Lexi hummed a response, then turned to look out the window for the rest of the drive. Which was fine by me. I don't think my heart could take any more Lexi time, especially sweet and soft and encouraging Lexi time. I was ready to back off and go to bed.

But then when we got to the house, she hopped out of my car and landed on her foot wrong. She yelped and in a matter of seconds, I was by her side and leaning down to check her ankle. She looked fine, of course she did, but still ... I scooped her up and walked her to the door.

"Woah, Kay, it's not that big of a deal. You can put me down," she squealed.

"It's probably not a big deal, but still ... I'll put you down on the couch and grab you some ice."

"Seriously?"

"Yes. Seriously." I jostled her a little as I moved to open the door. Setting her down on the couch before turning on one of the table lights. I took a glance up the stairs to confirm that my parents' room was already dark and turned to Lexi, finger on my lips. "Don't get up."

I retrieved an ice pack and glass of water from the kitchen and came back to find Lexi strewn across the couch, arm over her face. I set the water on the coffee table and sat at the end of the couch, pulling her feet into my lap and taking off her shoes. She mumbled something, but laying down must've revealed how tired she was, so I just kept going, cuffing her jeans and removing her socks.

"Are you undressing me Kaleb Russel?" she murmured, peeking up at me from under her arm.

"I'm checking for swelling. It's easier to tell if I can compare the two." If she thought removing her socks counted as undressing her, what did she think of me taking my hoodie back? Because that felt a hell of a lot more intimate than what I was doing now. This was business, this was something I'd trained for, that was … something else.

I held both her feet up, massaging around her ankles and then up her legs slightly.

"So how is it doc? Am I gonna live?"

"Well, you're not swelling yet, but that doesn't mean anything. Ice it for 15 minutes and drink that water." I stood up, propping her foot up on a pillow before placing the ice on it.

"What's the water for?"

"The hangover you'll have tomorrow. I'll grab you some ibuprofen, that'll help with any swelling too." When I returned with the meds, and some toast, Lexi was looking at her phone with narrowed eyes.

"What's up?" I asked, handing her the plate and meds.

"Nothing." She accepted the plate, taking the meds without water.

"Yeah, then why're you glaring at your phone? Also, you should take medicine with a full glass of water." She rolled her eyes at me, setting her phone aside to drink. I sat back at her feet, peeking under the ice to see if her skin had reddened.

"Apparently Jay kept singing your praises after we left, so now all my girl friends are asking me if you're single," she finally said.

"Oh." I was kind of taken aback, but not surprised. Jay had a big mouth and liked to exaggerate things, especially when he drank. He was probably trying to make it look like I was a man whore to make the girls uninterested in me, but it backfired. But I was more concerned about the tightness in Lexi's calf.

"Are you?"

"What?" I looked up from her leg to see she'd sat up, propped against some pillows, eyes narrowed at me.

"Single?"

"Oh, yeah, I am. But if I'm being honest, I'd rather you not tell any girls asking about it. I'm not trying to hook up with anyone at the wedding. Could you imagine the fit Blake would throw?" With that addressed, I returned my attention to her calf, messaging her leg through her jeans. This wasn't the best angle to work out her tension, but I didn't want to cross a line and ask her to lay on her stomach. If I just pressed a little more, it should help.

"Oh," Lexi said, her voice almost a moan, and I looked up to see her eyes rolling to the back of her head, mouth opened. And that was an image that shot straight to my dick.

Shit, I forgot most people didn't get massages regularly and when they did it was from a partner. I held my breath, pulling my hands away from her as I waited for Lexi's response. When her eyes returned to me, she blushed and immediately looked away.

"Sorry, I wasn't expecting a massage. Is that part of your bedside treatment you're learning in school?"

"Sort of. I mean, medical massages are a little different, but there are similarities." I swallowed, getting up and trying to adjust my body's reaction to the sound of her moaning. "But I'm gonna go to bed. Keep icing for ten more minutes and be careful when you go up the stairs. Oh and try to keep it elevated while you sleep, I know that's a hard ask, but –"

"Okay, okay, go to bed already, Mr. Worrywart. It doesn't even hurt."

"And it won't if you do what I say." I meant to add caution to my words, but I couldn't help but smile and that just made it sound like I was teasing her. But she smiled in response, waving me away. So I went up to bed with a smile on my lips.

CHAPTER 6

Lexi

After unnecessarily icing my leg, taking medicine, and eating toast, I quietly ascended the stairs of the Russel family home, thinking more about Kaleb and his fingers than I had in my entire life. The light was still on in his room as I passed by and I almost considered knocking to ask him to work out a whole different kind of tension. Almost. But despite the drinks, I still had my wits about me. So I changed and snuggled up in Blake's bed, unsatisfied.

Me: Gonna flick the bean in your childhood bed, Blake.

Blake: Ew.

Kat: Ew.

Blake: TMI Lex. But go for it, I guess.

Me: Who said I was asking for permission?

Blake: Ew times infinity.

Kat: What's got you so hot and

bothered?

Like hell I was answering that.

> **Blake:** My punk ass brother gave her too many drinks. She always gets horny when she drinks rum. Don't you remember that Alpha Kappa party where I had to pull her off of some frat dude?
>
> **Kat:** Oh right. But Kaleb didn't know that. He was just trying to take care of Lex.
>
> **Blake:** He knows what it means to buy a woman a drink. Intentions aside, he's still a punk.
>
> **Me:** Are you guys sitting side by side while texting?

In response, Blake sent a picture of him and Kat in their PJs, tucked into their hotel bedroom, both wearing extremely cheesy smiles. Disgusting.

> **Me:** Y'all are cute, but not what I'm in the mood to see. Night. See y'all tomorrow.

I sat in silence for a moment, staring at the wall Kaleb was on the other side of. Then I opened up a new message just to Kat.

> **Me:** Go to the bathroom or something, I need to talk to you without Blake seeing your screen.
>
> **Kat:** 'Kay.

She was silent for a moment, but Blake immediately filled that silence with his own private message.

> **Blake:** Why did you make my fiancé go to the bathroom? Are you talking about her bachelorette party? Wedding stuff?
>
> **Me:** Wedding stuff.
>
> **Me:** Wedding undergarment stuff.
>
> **Blake:** Very good, continue.

We'd picked out her wedding night outfit before Blake had even proposed, but he definitely didn't need to know that.

> **Kat:** Okay, I'm squared away. What's up? And please tell me it has to do with how you were looking real flustered after talking with Kaleb outside.
>
> **Me:** KAT!!!
>
> **Kat:** It is, isn't it? I'm so smart.
>
> **Me:** HE PINNED ME AGAINST THE WALL AND ASKED IF I SAW HIM AS A MAN!!!!!!
>
> **Kat:** Smooth moves, Kaleb.
>
> **Kat:** Don't leave me hanging, what did you say? Are you gonna be my sister-in-law? That'd be pretty cool, not gonna lie.
>
> **Me:** Too far.
>
> **Me:** And I just said that I could see him as a man now.
>
> **Me:** And I sort of pushed my hips into him. And felt him.

Kat: !!!

Me: Don't you dare tell Blake.

Kat: Oh god no, he'd have a fucking conniption. I mean, it'd be pretty funny, but not worth the trouble unless you guys end up being a real thing.

Me: Kat, what am I gonna do? I stumbled out of his car and he sorta freaked out, not like in a bad way, but in a let's-make-sure-you-didn't-hurt-yourself way. He made me ice my ankle! I literally just stepped funny and he insisted I go full on RICE routine. Then he massaged my calf! And I moaned! I repeat, what do I do?!?!

Another message from Blake popped up.

Blake: Why is my future wife giggling so hard? Are you making fun of me in there?

I immediately dismissed him without response.

Kat: Well, you were planning on masturbating anyways, right? Just go ahead with that and cry his name loud enough so that he can hear from his room. Then maybe he'll come over and help you out.

Me: Kat, I need serious suggestions here. I can't just fuck Blake's brother. I've known him since he was like a baby.

Kat: Well he's not a baby anymore. And he's got amazing hands.

Me: Wait, how do you know that?

Kat: When I was there for Christmas, Kaleb wanted to practice his massage technique. Apparently he took some extra classes with an actual masseuse because he wanted to know both sides of massaging.

Kat: It wasn't sexual, if you're jealous. He's a proper professional and diligent student.

Me: Shut up. I know. When he asked me if I saw him as a man, his eyes were ... I dunno. But when he was massaging my leg, I didn't get those vibes at all. He definitely wasn't doing it to come on to me.

Kat: Okay, backtrack, after you leaned into him, what happened?

Me: He backed up like I scared him!

Kat: Aw, how cute!

Me: How is that cute? I scared him!

Kat: I don't think you scared him. I mean, you're an older woman, sort of off-limits, he probably just didn't expect you to respond like that.

Me: I shouldn't have responded like that.

Kat: But?

Me: No but! I should just keep it in my pants.

Kat: If you say so. But don't come crying to me when he hooks up with someone at the wedding.

Kat: But also, if you were just attracted to the wall pinning thing, then you should definitely leave it alone. I don't want you breaking little Kaleb's heart.

Me: Me?

Kat: Yeah you. Have you ever had a thing go on for more than a month?

Me: ... No.

Kat: Exactly. You get attracted to a guy, get together to feed that desire, then hurt yourself because he isn't what you really want. Honestly, I blame Blake. He fulfills your need for male companionship, so you only go to other men for sex. Don't use Blake for sex.

Kat: *****Kaleb. Don't use KALEB for sex. I'M the one using Blake for sex.

Me: I wouldn't do that.

Kat: Good.

Kat: That said, if you did catch real, honest to god feelings, Kaleb would be a good option for you.

Me: Yeah, all right, I'm done with this conversation. Go have fun with your future hubby.

Kat: Will do! You have fun masturbating to the thought of Kaleb pinning you to a wall again!

Kat's warning was right. If I was just attracted to the way Kaleb acted tonight in the heat of the moment, then I should just stay away until my body cooled down. But I wasn't just attracted to the way he pinned me against the wall. I was attracted to his consideration and gentleness tonight too. And those fingers made me just as hot and bothered as the way he gently pulled his hoodie off me.

So I gave in, made myself comfortable, and nude from the waist down, and closed my eyes. I pictured Kaleb leaning over me on the couch, his eyes hungry like they'd been at the bar, scanning down my naked body so slowly I shivered. He'd moan, murmuring something about how he's wanted to do this for years, and kiss me tenderly, slowly, until I wrapped my arms around his neck and pulled him closer because I want more. And he'd give me what I want because it didn't take much imagination to see that Kaleb would be just as giving and attentive to my needs in my sex fantasy as he was in real life.

While we kissed, Kaleb's free hand would travel down my body, massaging small circles into my skin. But he wouldn't touch me where I wanted, not where it counted, not yet. Why was it that I imagined Kaleb as a tease? But no, tease wasn't the right word for what I imagined. I imagined him going over every inch of my body, massaging me so that I was completely relaxed. Because what he was going to do to me later would require my body to be ready. And god, those hands. I'd only felt them briefly on my ankle, then through my jeans, but his touch was just the right amount of pressure to make my body melt under him. The sounds I would've made if he'd touched me elsewhere.

Fantasy Kaleb moved away from my lips, kissing a trail down to my breasts. I arched my back so that my nipple reached his mouth quicker and he stopped his kisses to look at me with a crooked smile, his eyes sparkling. "I'm glad you aren't afraid to ask for what you want."

Well, yeah, fantasy Kaleb, this was a fantasy after all. But thinking about it now, I don't think I would be afraid to ask him for anything. You had to be responsive to somebody's body to be a good masseuse, right? And Kat had shared some things about Blake in bed. Russel men *wanted* to give you everything. Or at least I thought so. I couldn't tell if I got that idea from a vibe I got off Kaleb or if it was just what I wanted to read given the information I had.

Fantasy Kaleb drew my attention back to him as he kissed around my nipple, his touch like butterfly wings. I'd lean into him more and he'd chuckle at my desperation, putting his knee in between my legs so that when my hips raised, my clit would graze against him. His tongue started grazing over my breast, trailing over my nipple then flicking it twice before sucking down.

His leg between mine would nudge my legs to the

side and I'd open for him eagerly. His fingers would massage my thigh slowly and I'd groan impatiently. "Don't worry, baby, I'll get there. I just want to savor every inch of you."

When his fingers finally reached my center, he'd take one long stroke over me before his thumb rested on my clit, using those small massage circles and gentle pressure to make every single one of those nerve endings cry out in relief. "Does that do it for you, baby?"

I wouldn't be able to reply, just whimper as warmth flooded over me and my body convulsed underneath him. But Kaleb, fantasy Kaleb, wouldn't be assured by just that response. He'd want me to say it out loud. So his mouth would leave my breast and his hand would move to rest on my thigh. "Do you want more from me?"

Fuck. Yes, I did. I'd whimper his name, beg, whatever it took for him to touch me more. And he'd obliged, but not before taking my arms and pinning my wrist above my body. He lined up our hips, pressing so that his head rested at my opening. He leaned into my neck and nibbled at my ear. "I wanna slam into you, baby, is that okay?"

Yes, fuck yes, that's exactly what I want. He'd smile, pushing my legs further apart, before slamming into me. And fuck, to be full of him, full of that hard cock I'd gotten just a hint of. It'd be fucking fantastic. Especially with his weight pinning me down. Fuck. "God, baby, how are you more perfect than my dreams? You're gorgeous, Lex, absolutely stunning writhing on my cock. Everything I've wanted and more. Tell me you want me too, baby, please."

Shit, that was it. My body caught up to the fantasy, shaking as I fell over the edge thinking about Kaleb's desire for me, the perfect overwhelming sense of being wanted. And I really wanted Kaleb to want me, every bit of me.

Fuck. I took a deep breath, grabbed some tissues to clean up, then got myself ready for bed. And I definitely wasn't going to fall asleep to the thought of Kaleb asking if I wanted him. Or how my heart had a definitive answer.

CHAPTER 7

Kaleb

I woke up at the crack of dawn to take a jog so that I didn't risk seeing my parents or Lexi. But more importantly, so that I could burn off some of the energy that was winding me up. I should've just jacked off last night, but when I heard Lexi pass my door, the closeness made me choke. So I spent a restless night thinking about how her skin felt and how small she looked in my hoodie and how I hoped she was keeping her ankle elevated.

When I got to the house, I was still restless. Restless and sweaty. So the first thing I did, after making sure Lexi was still asleep, was hop into the shower. Alone and with enough space that my body demanded some relief.

So I rested my head on the shower wall and stroked myself, thinking about what would've happened if I'd kissed her at the bar after she'd leaned into me instead of backing away like a scared kid. If I'd kissed her, she would've moaned the way she did when I rubbed her leg. And she'd pull away from me, her eyes sobered and surprised, at me, at herself. Then *she* would kiss me, wrapping her arms around my neck and pulling me closer to her. I would try to go slowly, but Lex wouldn't let me, she'd demand more. Our tongues would slide against each other and suddenly my fingers were tangled up in her hair, pulling her closer, matching her intensity. And she'd murmur my name, pushing her whole body against me. Her breasts against my chest, my hard dick against her hip, and moans sounding from both of us. "Kaleb, please."

And damn, I'd give her anything she wanted. I let my fantasy fast forward to us in my bedroom. She'd stand there, arms raised, letting me pull off her clothes, my fingertips grazing her newly exposed skin. Taking off my hoodie from her yesterday had boiled my brain. I was focusing so hard on not accidentally pulling up her shirt, that I didn't notice how hard my dick was twitching at the thought of it, revolting at the sheer thought of not taking the chance to touch her.

But I didn't hold back in my fantasy. I wanted to touch every inch of her, feel her warmth against my hands, and make her feel *good*. And since I already knew one way to do that, I laid fantasy Lexi on my bed and massaged every inch of her, worshiped her. I avoided the parts I wanted to touch most, because I wanted to make her feel good, feel relaxed, make her feel like she needed my hands on her, needed me by her side the way I needed her. And when the need finally became too much for her, she'd whine, "I need your cock inside me."

Not yet, baby. I'd get down on my knees, spreading her legs wide so I could get a full view before leaning in for a taste. Fuck. Just one lick and she'd start shaking, begging me for more, to not stop. And if she tasted half as good as I imagined, I'd never want to stop. I'd suck on her clit before sliding my fingers into her. She'd curl her fingers into my hair, tight, and thrusting her hips up into me, making those pathetic little whines. "Kaleb, I –"

She wouldn't be able to finish that sentence, the words would fall, just like she fell over the edge. And the taste of her, god damn. Making her come would be the greatest honor of my life, watching her come undone by my hand. Fuck.

"Kaleb?"

Shit. That wasn't fantasy Lexi. That was real Lexi standing outside the bathroom, calling my name, just as I came on the shower wall. Shit. Did I come from her voice or was it just a coincidence?

"Kaleb?" she called again.

"Yeah?" I croaked out the word, flustered as I cleaned up the wall.

"Can I come in? I forgot to take out my contacts last night and my eyes are killing me."

"Um, sure." Idiot, idiot, idiot. I just couldn't say no to her, could I? Didn't matter that there might be a smell. Didn't matter that the shower door was completely see-through. She needed something, like hell I was gonna keep her from it.

I heard the door creek open and I instinctively turned away. Better for her to see my ass than my dick.

"Sorry, I'll be super quick. I just woke up and realized my eyes had shriveled up like raisins."

Her voice was a little rough from having just woken up, and possibly from last night's drinks. It was cute.

"How's your head and your ankle?" I asked, shifting in the shower to keep my back to her while I rinsed off any remnants of soap and come. She didn't respond and I looked over my shoulder to see her squinting at the mirror, her fingers plying at her eyes. Taking advantage of her lack of vision, I turned off the shower and cracked the door so I could grab my towel.

Dry and covered, I stepped out to see Lexi had put her glasses on. She looked over to me and I thought I saw her blush as she turned back to the mirror.

"I'm good, thanks. Though I do think you were being too cautious about my ankle."

I looked down to her foot, squinting as if I could see any swelling from here. But of course I couldn't and since she had the bachelorette party tonight, I wanted to make sure she was okay before she went out.

"Hop up on the counter and let me see."

"What?" Her voice was a squeak, high pitched in comparison to her sleepy voice. I squinted my eyes at her, trying to figure out what I'd done to make her react that way.

"I wanna make sure there's no swelling."

"Oh, right, sure. But I'm telling you, it's nothing."

She hopped up on the counter, the sleep shorts riding up her thighs as she settled onto the marble counter. I knelt down and focused on her ankles, comparing the feel of her tendons.

"Did you do what I asked you to last night?" I looked up to meet her eyes, but I found myself caught by the way her chest moved with heavy breaths.

"What?" Lexi asked and this time I managed to meet her eyes and she was looking at me like ... like a woman who *wanted*. But she also looked a little embarrassed with herself, face flushed as she bit her lips.

"Did you elevate your foot?" I choked out.

"Oh ... yeah, no, I didn't do that. But is it even swollen?" She laughed, covering her mouth as she did. I let her feet go and stood back up. Why was I making such a big deal of a misstep? Was it just an excuse to touch her?

"No, it looks fine. But still, wear sneakers to the bachelorette if you can. Flats at the very least." She rolled her eyes at me and slid off the counter, landing just inches from where I stood. She was close enough that I could feel her breath tickle my chest hair and blood rushed to my head, both ways.

"Um, bathrooms all yours." And I got the hell out of there before my towel exposed me.

CHAPTER 8

Lexi

I was ready for Kat's bachelorette party three hours early. Why? Because being around Kaleb was starting to drive me crazy. Especially after the bathroom fiasco. Our second bathroom fiasco in two days. I should've just waited and suffered in silence.

I can't believe I jacked off to Kaleb last night. And I can't believe I checked out his ass while he was innocently showering. But damn, it was a nice ass.

And now, I can't be in the same room as him without feeling flustered. I was never gonna get over this attraction if I kept seeing him in different states of undress.

"Lex?" Kaleb called from the other side of the bedroom door. Swallowing a lump in my throat, I got up from Blake's bed and opened the door. Kaleb's eyes met mine, then immediately flashed to my sneakers, a small smile pulling at his lips, like he didn't want me to see that he was happy I'd listened to him.

"I just wanted to ask if you needed a ride to Kat's

party." He looked back up to me, a hand running through his curls as he leaned against the door frame.

"Oh, did Blake ask you to do that? I don't want you to feel obligated to chauffeur me around all this week." He squinted at me, tilting his head.

"Blake didn't ask me to. I want to. You shouldn't have to take a cab when I'm available to drive you."

Oh. I could feel my heart pull towards him at that, that sweet caring tenderness.

"I don't want you to have to wait around for me though. The party will probably go on pretty late."

"I don't mind," he said with a shrug and I got the feeling that no matter what I said, he wasn't going to take no for an answer. And unlike some guys I've dated, his instance was about helping me, not using me. And that felt … nice.

No, no, no. I wasn't thinking about how Kaleb made me feel. He was just doing the polite thing, I'm a guest and a friend, he's being courteous. But wait, did he even consider me a friend? We were friendly before I left for college, but more like acquaintance friendly. That sort of friendship would fade after a year, and we hadn't really talked in ten. I only felt close to him because I saw him on social media and Blake would always come back from family holidays with stories. That was closer to my feelings for John Mulaney than an actual friendship.

"Can I take that as a yes?" Kaleb asked, filling the silence I had left by questioning where our relationship stood, pre-horny feelings.

"If you really don't mind, sure."

"I don't, I promise." He paused, smiling down at me, his eyes soft. I desperately wanted to know what he was thinking and I especially wanted to know what he thought about me. But he shifted in the doorframe and said, "It's still a bit before the party, right? Are you eating there? We could go grab a bite now, if you want."

Kat's bachelorette party was going to be in a private booth in a club. There'd be finger food, but mostly drinks. And if last night was any indication of how much I'd thirst after Kaleb when I was tipsy, getting some food in me now sounded like a good idea. God forbid he picks me up wasted and I jump him.

"That's a good idea, let's go."

❀ ❀ ❀

Friendliest was a diner that had been open since I was a little kid and it was just as busy now as it was on opening day. The story is some rich, ex-politician was sick and tired of franchises opening up in town, namely the Friendly's that had once been a block away, so he gave a chef friend the funds to open the diner. His only condition was that the restaurant couldn't become a big franchise and it had to be a play on Friendly's.

"Table for two?" the hostess asked when we stepped inside, but then her customer service smile softened as she looked up to Kay. "Oh hey Kaleb."

"Hey, Angie. How're you doing?" Kaleb asked. I looked the woman over, thinking she'd be someone I might remember from high school, somebody's little sister, or something. But she didn't look like anyone I knew. She had long, straight black hair and a very pretty smile. And then I saw her name tag and it clicked in place. This was Angela. The girl Kaleb left with from one of Jay's parties. Huh.

"Eh, I'm all right, all things considered. Table's this way." Angela pulled out two menus and guided us to the back of the restaurant, setting our menus down at the corner booth. She placed a hand on Kaleb's back as he passed her to sit down. And I didn't miss that wistful smile she had when she walked away.

"What's that about?" I asked, the words slipping out of me before I had a chance to think about how dumb they sounded.

"What do you mean?"

"Oh, you guys just seemed ... close, I guess."

"Really? I mean, we went out a couple times in high school, but we haven't really talked since then." Kaleb cleared his throat and shuffled in the booth uncomfortably. Well I guess that was a sign he didn't want to talk about it. I guess that was fair, I didn't exactly want to talk about my failed relationships either.

"Okay. Um, do you come here a lot when you're back home?" That should be a safe subject, right?

"Not really. The only friend I still have in town is Jay and he's ... well you know, not really a friend. But I came here a lot during high school. You guys did too, right?" He didn't look at me as he spoke, his eyes focused on the menu.

"Yeah. Dinner food is always the best after a drink."

"Guess we've got the order mixed up." He chuckled, looking up to meet my eyes with an infectious smile. Then he cleared his throat and looked back down. "We've talked about my job, it's your turn."

"Ugh, I'm on vacation. Do I really have to talk about work?" I groaned and he chuckled again.

"It's only fair."

"Fine, fine. I write proposals. So like, a big long paper explaining why my company can do a job and how we'd be the best at it and shit."

"And shit? So it's safe to say you hate your job?"

"Hate is a strong word. I like my coworkers, I like my manager, to a certain extent, and I get paid well enough. So I'm not exactly inclined to find something else that I *really* like, you know?" Kaleb nodded along as I spoke, his eyes thoughtful. And I was suddenly worried that he was going to give me the advice everybody who loved their job gave.

"Yeah, there's no shame in that. Money is money. If you can make it doing something you love, great, but not everybody has that luxury. Plus, it's not like you can't quit at any time if you find something you want to do."

My shoulders instantly relaxed at his words, his assurances, and I smiled.

"Thanks, I ... I needed to hear that."

He looked over to me, his chest still, licking his lips like he was about to say something. But a sleepy teenager interrupted us with a loud fake cough.

"What can I get for you?" the kid said.

"You ready to order, Lex?" Kaleb asked, fingers toying with the edge of the menu. Did he pick up the vibe that the kid thought we were an annoying couple too or was that just me? Or maybe I was just projecting what I wanted.

"Oh yeah, can I get the french toast, a side of hash, and an iced mocha?" The kid nodded as he scribbled in a pad, then turned to Kaleb.

"And can I get the lumberjack, another side of hash, a side of bacon, and a strawberry milkshake."

"Ooo, milkshakes. Do you guys have cookies and cream?" I asked, a little more excitedly than I should have. The kid sighed but nodded.

"Do you want that in addition to or instead of the coffee?" he mumbled.

"In addition to, thanks."

"Coming right up." The kid shuffles away, barely picking up his feet as he headed towards the kitchen. I turned back to see Kaleb smiling at me and I felt my cheeks warm up.

"What?"

"Nothing, just … you sure you wanna drink all that before you go out drinking?"

"Oh, shit, I didn't think about that. It'll be fine, I'll just pee before we leave. And if you wanna talk over ordering, what about you? Isn't the lumberjack the biggest meal on the menu?"

"Yeah, but it doesn't come with bacon and hash, it comes with sausage and diced potatoes."

"Couldn't you just ask to substitute them?" I asked through a laugh, which seemed to be contagious because he was starting to laugh at himself too.

"I could, but I want sausages *and* bacon."

"And the potatoes?"

"I didn't have lunch."

✳ ✳ ✳

"Good, I'm so full. I'm gonna have to dance the whole night to work off this food," I said when we were back in the car and on the way to Kat's party. Beside me Kaleb bit his lip, frowning. What was that about? Did he not like me talking about how much I ate or something? No, he watched me eat and we had fun, laughing and sharing stories. So that shouldn't be it.

"Be careful though, okay? Do you have ... pepper spray or something?"

"Pepper –" I started but couldn't help but laugh. Of course this boy was looking out for me. What else could I have thought was going on? "I don't think that'll be necessary. It's girls' night, no guys allowed."

"Oh good." His shoulders visibly relaxed, and he added, "But sexual assault isn't gender exclusive. So still watch your drinks."

"Yes, sir, I'll be careful. And if you're really worried, Kat always carries pepper spray and those little claw key chain things."

"And she's going to have them tonight?"

"I don't see why she wouldn't."

"Ask her."

"Okay, okay. Geez, you're the over protective type now, huh?" I pulled out my phone and opened up Kat's messages, then immediately tilted my phone away from Kaleb because we hadn't texted since last night. And those were messages I *did not* want Kaleb seeing.

> **Me:** Kat, text me a shit ton of messages.
>
> **Kat:** Lol, what're you trying to hide, huh?
>
> **Me:** Shut up and do it please.
>
> **Kat:** All right, fine, but you better tell me why when you get here. And your ass better be on the way.
>
> **Kat:** Fuck, it's so hard to think of shit to say like this.
>
> **Kat:** Oh, whatever you told Blake that we were doing, it made him super horny. As soon as I stepped out of the bathroom he pounced on me like he was starved and I was a turkey diner.
>
> **Me:** I want to be comfortably able to show Kaleb a text from you.

"Is everything okay? That's a lot of texting for one question."

"It's fine, I wasn't texting her. My mom had just asked me how the wedding stuff was going and I wanted to answer her first."

"Oh, okay. Are your parents not coming?"

> **Kat:**
> OOOOOOOOOOOOOOOOOOOOOOOO

"No. But they sent a Kitchen Aid mixer, so you know, all forgiven."

> **Kat:** Okay, okay, okay. Now I'm super excited to talk to you. Is he driving you here?
>
> **Me:** Yes, we're on our way now. We just ate at Friendliest.
>
> **Kat:** Sounds like you're getting pretty friendly. *winky face*

I'm going to murder her. But then she sends a flood of pictures of her and Blake, all sweet and innocent and pictures Kaleb has likely already seen on her Instagram.

> **Me:** Hey, Kaleb wants to know if you're bringing pepper spray. Apparently he's a feminist and says women can be assaulters too.
>
> **Kat:** I am and he's right.

"Kat *is* bringing pepper spray and she says you're right to worry about women assaulters." Kaleb took his eyes off the road to look at me, one eyebrow raised.

"And you're not just saying that to keep me from making a pitstop at whatever store sells pepper spray?"

"No, I can show you," I said, tilting my phone for him to see, but he turned back to the road without looking.

"Nah, I believe you. Just wanted to double check."

> **Me:** He didn't even look at my phone. What the fuck am I doing?
>
> **Kat:** Falling in love with a Russel

brother it sounds like.

Me: Kat!

Kat: Fine, you're not falling in love with him.

Me: Thank you.

Kat: You were already in love with him and you're just now realizing it.

Me: You're saying I was in love with him when he was 14?

Kat: Ok, I stand corrected. I'll stick with you falling in love with him.

"Here we are," Kaleb said and I looked up to see the glowing neon sign of Drinks. As clever a name as Friendliest, I guess. The brick building was lined with women in a wide variety of attire, from sparkly short dresses to plain jeans and T-shirts.

Kaleb pulled up to the curve, looking over his shoulder before putting on the flashers and getting out. He opened my door, holding my hand as I got out. And Kat was absolutely wrong. I wasn't falling in love. I was just a little attracted to my best friend's brother. Just a little. And maybe my heart fluttered around him. But just a little.

"Call me when you're ready to leave. And be careful, okay?"

"Okay, okay, I will." And god, I must've lost my mind for a moment, because as I spoke, I went up on my tiptoes, held his bicep to keep balance, and kissed him on the cheek. And when I settled back down to the ground, I was too embarrassed to see how he reacted and immediately skittered to the entrance.

It was just a kiss on the cheek. Just a kiss on the cheek. That's nothing. That's something his mom would do or a sister, if he had one. Heck, Kat might've kissed him on the cheek before. But I hadn't. Because it never had felt natural before. But he'd just treated me to dinner and drove me to this party. So I kissed him, on the cheek, as, like, a thank you. That was it.

CHAPTER 9

Kaleb

It was nothing, just a kiss on the cheek, nothing more. But damn, it felt right. Like I was always taking her out on dates and then dropping her off to have fun with friends.

Because today felt like a date. She told me about her job and shared something that felt like an insecurity, an insecurity that didn't seem to bother her anymore after we talked. And we laughed and talked about old times and the things we'd done since she last came to town. And I didn't feel like a kid. Lexi looked at me like an equal. And it did feel good when that teenager looked at us like we were an annoying couple.

And then she kissed me. On the cheek. And it probably meant nothing to her. It was a thank-you-for-dinner-and-driving-me kiss. A kiss you gave your friends. A kiss you gave your best friend's kid brother.

No, she definitely didn't think of me as a kid anymore. If she did, I don't think she would've kissed me at all since she'd never done it before.

Right. This was good, this was progress. This is exactly what I wanted.

But what the hell was I gonna do when I pick her up? Should I kiss her on the cheek too? Stick with a hug?

My phone rang and without looking I answered it on speaker, worried Lexi had somehow gotten into trouble. But it was my brother's voice that came through the stereo.

"Hey, kiddie Kay! What're you doing?"

"Wow, you went, what? Ten minutes without Kat before you got bored?"

"Ouch. Give me a little credit. It took 20. What're you doing?"

I contemplated not telling him that I went out with Lexi and then dropped her off at the party. But the likelihood that Kat would mention it was high. Plus we might run into each other on pickup, so I told the truth. Most of the truth.

"I just dropped off Lexi at the bachelorette party."

Blake was very quiet for a long while and I held my breath.

"You didn't have to do that, bro. She could've taken a cab."

"You're the one who told me to be her DD yesterday."

"Well that was because you were both coming to the party and we both know you would've done it even if I hadn't asked you too."

This time I was quiet. Because he was right and he

knew exactly what that meant.

"Look, I'm sorry I got on your ass about Lex yesterday. I just ... well I know you've had a crush on her for forever and --"

"I have not," I said instinctively and I could picture him rolling his eyes.

"Sure you haven't. But you were definitely feeling some type of way last night. And you *and* Lex have shit dating history. I don't want to see that fall out."

"What do you mean by that?"

"What? The fall out or the dating history?"

"The dating history."

"Well, you haven't had a steady girlfriend, ever. I swear, you're tagged in a pic with a new girl every week. Which, like, that's all cool, if they're cool with it, but Lexi's not like that."

"I could be in a steady relationship," I argue, even though Blake is the last person I want to have this conversation with. I hadn't had a steady girlfriend because I'd spent my whole life hung up on Lexi. If a girl asked me out, I gave her the "I'm not looking for anything serious" speech and when things changed for her and not me, we broke up. I felt bad about it, at one point I'd hoped against all odds that I'd catch feelings, but I never did.

"Sure you can. But either way, that doesn't solve Lexi's issue, which is dating hot jackasses that treat her like shit"

"What?" I felt my breath catch in my throat, a series of bad scenarios running rampant in my head.

"Slow your roll, I can hear the panic in your voice already. They didn't hit her or anything, just like, ignored her calls, made her feel insecure, that kind of shit. You know I got her out of there the second I saw a red flag. But she didn't introduce me to every guy she dated. Sometime in our junior year, when Kat and I started going out, she went out a lot and I don't think she did it for the fun of it."

"Should I go back and get her?" I asked, worrying that maybe the drinking environment would be bad for her, but Blake just laughed.

"No, she'll be fine, Kat's with her and it's a girls' only night. But I'm telling you this because I don't want you to even think about messing with her. She needs someone who is a hundred percent into her, not someone who's idealizing her because of his childhood crush."

That's not what I was doing, right?

"And I guess you deserve to find someone like that for you too, blah, blah, blah. Kat would give me hell if she found out I scolded you about going after Lexi without telling you to find happiness elsewhere."

"Yeah, she's a good woman. You don't deserve her."

"I absolutely agree. So, you're gonna pick Lexi up after the party, right? What're you doing in the meantime?"

"Well, my old gym is in the neighborhood. So I figured I could squeeze a workout in."

"Perfect, see you there."

CHAPTER 10

Lexi

Two drinks in and I had still managed to avoid talking to Kat about what had happened between me and Kaleb. Because there was nothing to talk about. A kiss on the cheek was nothing. Except for the fact that I had felt the scruff on his cheek and, for the briefest of seconds, wanted to feel it on my thighs.

So no, there was nothing I needed to talk to Kat about. No matter how hard she stared at me while our friends yapped her ears off.

"Lexi, Lexi, tell us about Kaleb!" Rachel, a friend from college, begged, the other girls around us nodding in agreement with her plea.

"What about him?"

"You two aren't a thing, right? What's he like? Is he seeing anyone?"

I looked at Kat in a panic, but she just raised an eyebrow and kept drinking her champagne. We were sitting on a semicircle couch on the top floor of the club, Kat on the other end than I was, and every single one of the girls leaned in towards me, some setting their drinks down on the table.

"Um, we're not a thing. And he's … I dunno, I've known him since he was like, ye high. He's a good kid, a gentleman, I guess. And he did say he was single, but I don't really know his type or anything, if that's what you're asking. He didn't seem interested in finding anyone at the wedding though." God, I couldn't have stumbled over my words more than I just did. But no one seemed to notice or care, because as soon as I was done talking, they all turned to Kat expectantly.

"I wouldn't get your hopes up ladies, he's sort of a serial dater," she said, setting down her glass, crossing her arms, and looking directly at me.

"Really?" everyone said, myself included. Because the idea of that sweet boy flitting from girl to girl didn't make sense. Kat raised an eyebrow at me and sank back into the couch.

"Yeah. I'm pretty sure he's never had a serious girlfriend or anything. He's asked me for advice on girls before, mostly how to not hurt their feelings when they fell in love but he didn't."

"Well who could blame them? That body! Those dimples!"

"He's a certified masseuse too," Kat added, picking her glass back up and raising it to me.

All the girls groaned in response and Kat laughed, probably at my paling face. Because the idea of these girls crawling all over Kaleb didn't sit right with me. Especially if they were just after his body. He deserves somebody who wants all of him, his sweet consideration and gentle assurances, all of it. Better yet, he really deserved someone who wouldn't take advantage of his kindness. Maybe that's why he never dated anyone serious. They always ended up just wanting sex or they took his kindness without giving anything in return. And I sure as hell knew how that felt.

The girls started talking more about Kaleb's body and how they wouldn't mind being a wedding fling. And I got up so fast, I almost fell over. Someone offered me a hand and held me up as I made my way out of the couch zone and then towards the bathroom. I stood at the sink, taking in my frizzy hair and flushed face.

"You're looking pretty flustered," Kat said as she stepped in, thankfully alone.

"I don't know what you're talking about," I murmured and started washing my hands so I had something to do.

"You're avoiding looking me in the eye."

"I kissed him on the cheek, okay?" I waited for a moment, expecting a response, but when I met Kat's eyes she just looked confused.

"So?"

"So I've never done that. But we practically went on a date and he drove me here and it just felt like the right thing to do. And now I feel weird about it." I covered my face and groaned.

"Wait, back up. You went on a date?"

"Practically. We *practically* went on a date. A few

hours before the party he asked if I needed a ride, he didn't really take no for an answer, not in a forceful, gross way, but in a let-me-take-care-of-you way. And when I gave in, he asked if I wanted to eat beforehand so I'd have food in my stomach before drinking."

"Aw, cute."

"No, it's not cute, it's ... okay it's cute. But what am I doing?"

"You're --"

"And don't say I'm falling in love." Kat rolled her eyes but moved closer so that she could wrap her arms around me.

"Okay, no jokes. I think you're thrown off by how grown up and attractive Kaleb is. I think he's a good guy, who treats you well, and I'm not implying that's because he likes you or anything, that's just a fact. And since you're not used to being attracted to guys who treat you well, you're even more thrown off and confused. Okay?"

I nodded, because I couldn't bring myself to answer without crying. God, I didn't deserve Kat. Sure she was a pain in the ass sometimes, but she always knew what to say when it really counted.

"And, and I say this with all the love in the world, not because I'm trying to push you in any direction, if you wanted to test the water with Kaleb, you wouldn't be betraying Blake's friendship or anything. He'd get over it, I'd make sure of that. So, like, do what feels right for you. Except for using him for sex. I'm still not on board with that. He's my lil brother now too, almost. Honestly, I kinda wanna squeeze his cheeks every time I see him. Is that weird? Is that how all sisters feel?"

I choked out a laugh and Kat squeezed me tighter. I shifted around to hug her back, nuzzling my face into her neck.

"Now, are you in the mood to keep drinking? Or do you wanna call Kaleb and show off to all the girls that he's at *your* beck and call?"

"Kat," I whined.

"That's not an answer."

"Um, drinks."

"That's my girl!"

✳ ✳ ✳

"Kaleb, come get me, please!" I cried into my phone, my voice whinier than I expected it to be. How much had I drunk since Kat's little pep talk? Six? More?

"Kaleb!" a few of the other girls cried, equally wasted.

"Already?" Kaleb asked. He sounded a little out of breath and there was loud music in the background. What was he doing? Was he in some other club with women dropping themselves at his feet?

"Ask her if Kat's ready to go too," Blake's voice called, even more out of breath than Kaleb. That made my club theory make less sense. The bachelor's party wasn't until tomorrow. Were they doing a guys only party?

"Did you hear that, Lex?" Kaleb asked.

"Huh, oh yeah. Kat, do you wanna go yet?" I turned to where Kat was dancing with one of her sorority sisters and she waved me off.

"No, she's staying."

"Kat's gonna party longer, Blake. I'll see you tomorrow. Lex, I'm on my way. I'll text you when I get outside. Sorry, if I --" But I didn't get to hear the rest of whatever Kaleb was trying to say because somebody bumped into me and my fingers slipped over the hang up button. I shrugged it off, if it was important, he'd tell me when he got here. No sense in calling him while he was driving.

I weaved through the crowd to kiss Kat goodbye, waving to others as I went. Then I made my way to the door. Kaleb was already there, parked and holding my door open. And the sight of him had my jaw hanging. I wasn't surprised that he was already there. I was surprised by the state of him. He wore loose gym shorts and an even looser muscle talk, the arm holes going all the way down to his waist, showing off sweaty muscles. His curls were dark and pinned to his forehead. So either he just came from a sex marathon, which didn't seem likely since he was with Blake, or he'd been at the gym, killing time while waiting for me to call.

"Hey, Kaleb!" some bridesmaids called from the door of the club, giggling when he waved to them with a confused, but polite smile.

I wanted to hop into his arms and kiss him, if only to keep those girls from fantasizing about him, even though I did the exact same thing last night. But

1) I didn't have the right to stave off any of Kaleb's perspectives ... suitors, and 2) I was drunk and not coordinated enough to pull that off. Though I bet Kaleb would catch me anyways.

"Hey," I said, stopping in front of him.

"Hey. Sorry I'm all sweaty, I meant to time it out so that I was getting out of the shower when you called." He held out his hand, helping me up into the car and leaning in to help with my buckle when I pulled the belt too fast and it latched. Once I was buckled in, he pulled back so our faces were inches apart, our breaths mingling. And then he kissed my cheek. A soft, quick peck that burned my skin. He stepped back out of the doorway, licking his lips as he closed my door and rounded to the driver's side.

We didn't say anything for a while as Kaleb drove away. But when we were halfway back, I started getting restless about wasting my alone time with him.

"Kay, will you kiss me?" And god, I must've sounded desperate or something, because he choked on nothing. And once he'd recovered, he gave me a wide eye, deer in headlights kind of look. Fuck. That kind of hurt. I had thought of him as Blake's little brother for so long, but he probably thought of me as just Blake's best friend. And just because I was starting to feel insanely attracted to him, doesn't mean his feelings had changed too.

"Ask me again when you're sober." His voice had deepened, the words seeming to catch in his throat. I leaned in towards him, pushing my breast together just a bit. Because I could get away with this behavior right now and I wanted to know if he was at least a little attracted to me.

"Does that mean you'd say yes if I wasn't drunk?"

Kaleb looked over to me, his eyes drifting from my face down to my breasts. His breath hitched and he looked away, shuffling in his seat. Bingo.

"It means, ask me when you're sober. And sit back, that's dangerous."

I did as I was told, moving to look at the window. Out of the corner of my eye, I saw Kaleb reach down to his crotch and adjust himself. And that made my blood rush to my head. Which was a bad combination with all the drinks.

I rolled down the window and stuck my head out. Immediately, Kaleb grabbed a handful of my shirt and pulled me back in.

"What the hell are you doing?"

"Sobering up." That made him groan and sigh all at one.

"Lex, when I say sober, I mean well rested, fed, and *zero* alcohol in your system. Christ." He let go of the back of my shirt and I turned to face him, pouting. I couldn't help it. I had too much to drink and I wanted some relief from the heat that Kaleb burned in me.

"Fine," I grumbled and turned back to rest my head on the edge of the window. "Will you at least massage my legs before sending me to bed? I ... danced a lot."

"Of course, Lexi. So long as you eat something, drink a glass of water, and take some medicine beforehand." I groaned in reply, but was satisfied with his demands. "Though it'd be better if you stretched it out first."

"Kaleb," I cried, suddenly not wanting to move and risking getting nauseous.

"Okay, okay, I'll massage you. Geez."

CHAPTER 11

Kaleb

Lexi Jacobs asked me to kiss her and I said no.
Lexi Jacobs asked me to *kiss* her and I said *no*.

It was the right thing to do, I didn't doubt that. What I was hung up about was whether her drunk request was drunk courage or drunk horniness.

I walked up the stairs of my childhood home with a plate of toast and meds and a glass of water, on my way to massage my childhood crush. What kind of fantasy was I living in?

But no, she just asked me to massage her legs, they probably hurt or something. So I was going to take care of her and then go to bed. But that got a whole lot harder when I opened Blake's door and she was laying on the bed in just a baggy shirt and underwear. She was propped up on her elbow, scrolling through her phone, but looked over her shoulder at me and smiled.

"Where're you pants, Lex?" I choked out and her

smile widened. She climbed out of the bed and took the plate and glass from me before sitting back down. She crossed her smooth, long legs and ate.

"I figured it'd be easier without them," she said through a bite, shrugging.

Right, so she was just horny drunk. That I could handle. If she was doing this because of liquid courage and I found out later when she'd already gotten together with another man, I'd kick myself in the ass forever.

She finished eating, took the medicine, and downed the water. Then, with the excitement of a child on Christmas, she shuffled back to lay in the bed. I sat on the bed beside her and opened Blake's bedside table to grab some lotion, which was almost certainly there for some less than wholesome reason. I poured the lotion in my hands, rubbing it together to warm it up. Then I took a deep breath and started at the top of her thigh, switching my thought process to working mode so I didn't stare at her ass peeking out from under her panties.

And everything was going fine, my focus held, until she started moaning. It wasn't like last night when the sound slipped out of her and she immediately stopped herself. She was letting the sounds come to her naturally without holding back. She had to be doing this on purpose, torturing me for turning her down earlier. But she knew I wasn't turning her down, not really. I could tell she knew by the way she ... *presented* herself to me, like she wanted to test if I was just brushing her off or being nice.

"Kay, I want your hands all over me," she moaned, making my hands pause. I took another deep breath, then another one before I could continue.

"Ask me again when you're sober."

"Is that all you're gonna say to me tonight?" God, she was a whiny drunk. Was she like this in bed too? Whining for me to do what she wants, touch her where she wants, give her that sweet relief.

No, now wasn't the time for that.

"When it comes to any sort of sexual requests? Yes, that will be all I say tonight, Lex. I'll take care of you in every other way, but not like that, not when you're drunk." And not when I didn't know if you wanted me or just a body.

She let out a loud huff as I added more lotion to my hands and moved to her other leg. For a moment, she was quiet and I started to wonder if my touch had changed somehow now that I was fighting a boner. But she must have been holding them in because when I hit the next pressure point she let out a big moan, shoving her face in the pillow.

"Lex, you have to be quiet. I don't think my parents would appreciate being woken up like this."

"This is torture, Kaleb." And I couldn't help it, I laughed.

"I know it is, Lex. God damn do I know. But I am going to finish massaging your legs so you're not sore tomorrow. And then we're both going to sleep. If you want to ask me for more tomorrow, when you're sober, you can. But if you don't, I'll just pretend you never said anything. Okay?" She murmured something into the pillow and nodded her head. I finished massaging her legs, and she seemed to at least attempt to not make any noise. Then I sent her to take out her contacts and when she was back, tucked her into bed.

CHAPTER 12

Lexi

I woke up to toast, medicine, and two glasses of water sitting on the bedside table. And a splitting headache.

I gulped everything down and sat up, very slowly, trying to remember what happened last night. I definitely didn't black out, but after Kat's pep talk in the bathroom, things started getting fuzzy. Kaleb picked me up, covered in sweat, then we talked about something. I got back to the room and put on PJs, except without pants so that Kaleb could ... massage my legs.

Fuck. Did I come on to him like some horny teenager?

I threw my head back to the pillow and groaned into my hands. I absolutely came on to him. There's no way I'd have asked for a massage if I wasn't trying to. How was I gonna face him now?

"Lex, you okay?" Kaleb asked from the other side of the door, with a soft knock. I sat up and pulled the covers over me. Which was a ridiculous reaction because 1) the door was closed and he wasn't going to open it unless I said to, and 2) even if he did open the door, I was wearing a shirt, there was nothing to cover. And I'm pretty sure he saw my ass in my underwear last night anyways.

"Um, yeah, I'm fine, thanks."

"Have you taken the medicine?"

"Uh-huh. I just did."

"Are you just getting up?"

"Yeah." Shit, how late was it? I fumbled over to get my phone from the bedside table and opened up a few dozen texts from Kat and the bridesmaids, their messages almost exclusively about Kaleb. But more importantly was the time. We had less than an hour till Blake's party.

God, what idiot thought it'd be a good idea to have a bachelor's party in the early afternoon? Me. What a dumbass.

"I'll be out in just a minute. Sorry!" I fumbled out of bed and grabbed the first outfit I put my hands on. Once dressed, I stopped in front of the mirror and tried to smooth my hair into something presentable. But what did it matter? We were about to go to a strip club. Who did I need to look good for?

* * *

The strip club was exactly what you'd expect from a club not in a big city. It was dark, somehow a little dusty, and very cold. Like seriously cold, how were the girls dancing when it was this cold? Was this intentional?

But whatever. This was Blake's party and he wanted to go to a strip club because that was the traditional bachelor party thing to do. So here we were. Me and a bunch of men, some of whom I barely knew, and one who I probably tried to jump last night.

The car ride here with Kaleb was awkward. He didn't say anything, but he also barely looked at me. And when he did, he looked … like he was waiting for something. And since I wasn't going to bring up my embarrassing behavior last night, I didn't say anything. So he spent most of the trip clutching the wheel until his fingers went white.

"Lex, isn't it, like, weird for you to be here?" Jason asked as we all settled down on the cushioned couch in front of the stage.

I wanted to tell Jason that it was weirder that he was here since he wasn't even a part of the wedding party. But I held that comment in.

"Nope, it's all good. I am fully capable of appreciating a beautiful woman."

"Yeah, she is!" Blake screamed, already three drinks in even though we'd just sat down. "When we went to Vegas a couple years ago, we went with Kat and it was awesome."

"You went with two girls?" one of the guys asked.

"Yeah, they didn't shut up about how powerful their legs must be."

"Well look at them. Can any of you hold yourself up on a pole like that?" I asked and they all shook their heads in response.

We didn't say much else as we watched the show, some of the guys hooted and hollered and tossed their money, but when I looked over to Blake, he was just staring off into space.

"What's up?" I asked, nudging Blake with my elbow.

"Eh, I'm kinda bored. This was more fun with Kat." Some of the guys crooned at him and called him whipped, but I just patted him on the shoulder.

"Wanna go ahead to the bar?" I asked.

"Yeah. Let's go after this song. Might as well let the single suckers have their fun."

"Sure." The two of us pulled out our phones while everyone else enjoyed the show.

Kat had texted me a few times since last night, mostly warnings about keeping it in my pants. How was I gonna tell her that I hadn't even managed to keep my pants on *and* that I didn't remember exactly what I said.

"Maybe it's being sober that's keeping you from enjoying the show," Jason said, handing Blake another beer. I rolled my eyes, but Jay had actually said something useful for once. The word sober triggered the memory of Kaleb saying, "Ask me again when you're sober." And he'd said it multiple times.

I pulled out my phone, ignored Kat's previous questions, and texted her.

> **Me:** What do you think it means when somebody says, "Ask me again when you're sober"?

Kat: Welcome back to the land of the living. And that depends on what was asked.

Me: But I don't know what I asked.

Kat: Wait, wait, wait!!!! Kaleb said that to you, didn't he? When you were drunk off your ass and horny? You absolutely asked for sex, you horn dog!

Me: You're not being helpful. And I don't remember what I was asking. He was kind of awkward this afternoon. He wasn't avoiding me though, so I couldn't have asked for that much, right?

Kat: Or you did and he was waiting for you to ask again so he could, in good conscience, say yes.

I put my phone away and looked for Kaleb down the couch of the bachelor party.

"Well at least one of us is having fun," Blake said with a chuckle, nudging me and pointing to where Kaleb was getting a lap dance. Her small hands lazily glazed over his shoulders as she moved her hips in slow circles. Then she took his hands to rest them on her hips, wiggle so that her breasts copied the motion. And Kaleb … well he didn't push her away. And when the woman leaned in to whisper something in his ears, he smiled awkwardly.

"I'm gonna head to the bar now, get us some drinks ready," I grumbled, my voice a little colder than

I intended as I shot up and fast walked to the door. If Blake said anything in reply, I didn't catch it.

The bar was just on the other side of the shopping center, but half way there someone grabbed my wrist. Kaleb. Looking slightly flushed like he'd run out after me.

"Are you okay? Were you uncomfortable?"

"Yeah, something like that," I scoffed, taking my hand back to cross my arms and cover my body, which was distinctly not like the stripper's. "But you looked like you were having fun, so go back, don't worry about me."

"Are you mad at me?" he asked, the hand that had been around my wrist flexing.

"Why would I be mad at you for getting a dance? That's kind of the whole point of the establishment." Was I mad? I don't even know, I just didn't want to see him enjoying another woman's body dancing all on him. That didn't mean I was mad. It meant I was jealous, which was way worse.

"Okay, well for someone who isn't mad, you sure sound irritated. And, not that you would care, I guess, but she dragged me away from the group. I didn't ask for it or anything."

"I'm not irritated. And you're all grown up, you can tell a woman no." And it sure seems like he told me no a lot last night.

"She was just doing her job."

"A job that you were enjoying." Why am I arguing with him about this? He didn't do anything wrong. I just … I wanted him to look at me like that and I was bitter that he wouldn't do anything to me last night. Because I was starting to remember him kissing my cheek and wanting more. I mean, logically, I knew he wouldn't do anything while I was drunk. But I wanted to feel wanted.

"Enjoying?" Kaleb repeated. And his eyes flitted to his crotch, as if to check that he wasn't pitching a tent. He wasn't. But that didn't mean anything, he was probably still turned on. "You're mad that my body responded to stimuli at a club *you* picked?"

"I told you I'm not mad."

"They're just sacks of fat, Lex, that's not enough to get me ..." Kaleb either thought better of what he was going to say or stopped because of the disgust and confusion on my face.

"Kaleb, did you just refer to that woman's breasts, her admittedly very nice breasts, as sacks of *fat*?" He put his hands in his pockets and shuffled his feet awkwardly.

"I didn't mean it as an insult, I was just trying to say that – I just don't want you mad at me, Lexi," he pleaded, looking down on me with puppy dog eyes like I'd just kicked him and he didn't know why. Of course he didn't know, I was being irrational. But I couldn't stop myself.

"I told you, I'm not mad. Now give me your keys," I said, holding out my hand. He pulled out his keys, staring at them for a second before looking at me with his brow furrowed.

"Why?" he asked, setting the keys in my outstretched hand.

"It's my turn to be DD tonight. So, you know, drink to your heart's content and have fun." I stuffed the keys in my pocket and spun away before Kaleb could argue with me or try and take his keys back.

"Lex!" he called as I finished making my way to the bar. But I didn't respond, I went in and ordered everyone's first round of drinks.

CHAPTER 13

Kaleb

Lexi was mad at me. Nothing she said convinced me otherwise. The way she stomped out of the club, huffing, was clue number one. Then she insisted she wasn't mad, rolled her eyes at me, and raised her voice. And the only reason I could think of was that she thought I was being disrespectful to the stripper. No, that's a lie, there's another reason she could be made, but I was going to be honest with myself and not let wishful thinking cloud my thoughts.

But I really didn't see how I could've disrespected the woman at the club. She was the one who talked to me, dragged me over to the armchair in the corner, and started dancing. I'd barely said anything to her. The whole time I was at the club, I was thinking about Lexi's ass and how it'd look dancing. And when the stripper said, "Let me take your mind off those worries," I let her. But I didn't touch her … well she put my hands on her waist, but that shouldn't count. And when she whispered to me, "This isn't working, huh?" I couldn't help but laugh. She was right, my head was so full of Lexi, that literally nothing could distract me from her.

And somehow, while I was replaying last night in my head over and over again and spacing out, I'd upset her. And her passive aggressive anger led her to take my keys and tell me to drink. I guess it was technically fair, but I didn't mind being her DD. And to be honest, I wouldn't have minded hearing her ask for me again. If I could just hear her one more time, I could live off that for the rest of my lonely life.

"Bro, drink up!" Jason cried, tilting my elbow up when I was taking a sip. I coughed on the beer and glared at Jay. I was not in the mood for his shit. But Lexi was avoiding me and I was going to let her. We'd talk about what was upsetting her when we got back home. For now, I'll give her space and drink. But I didn't want to get drunk. I wasn't like Lexi, but I definitely overshared when I had one too many.

"I'm gonna go grab another," I murmured to Jason and left the group for the bar. There, a woman around my age was looking exhausted while an older man in a suit blathered on and on. I stepped up beside them, reaching in between them to place my empty glass on the counter.

"Hey, sorry I'm late, got caught up on a work call as soon as I got here. I've been sitting at the other side of the bar for, like, 20 minutes. So I *was* technically on time, if that counts for anything," I said, not looking towards the man. The girl quirked her eyebrow but nodded.

"Yeah, I was just about to give up on you. Sorry, dude, but we've kinda got some stuff to talk about," she said. The man opened his mouth to say something, but when I wedged myself between them, he left. After the man was lost in the crowd, I waved the bartender over and ordered my drink.

"You want anything? I'll leave in a bit, just figure I should stick around in case he comes back."

"You don't have to do that."

"It's fine, consider it a sort of reparations." She laughed and ordered something. We sat in silence while we waited for our drinks and I kept my eye on the dude, who was thankfully heading to the door.

"Thanks, by the way, I owe you a favor ..." she said, trailing off as if she would have said my name if she knew it.

"Kaleb," I said and we shook hands.

"Sarah."

"And you don't owe me anything. All I really did was butt in." Our bartender set our drinks down and I grabbed mine then stepped away. "I'm here for my brother's bachelor party, which, you know, means we're just a group of drunk dudes. But if somebody bothers you again, you can hang out with us."

"Oh, thanks," she said as I was walking away. But then I met Lexi's eyes from across the bar and she snapped her gaze away and laughed at something Blake said.

"Actually, could I take you up on that favor?" I said, returning to Sarah's side at the bar.

"Oh no, was that whole thing just a tactic?" She grimaced at me, blue eyes narrowing.

"No, no, nothing like that. I just …" I looked back over my shoulder to Lexi and my heart dropped into my stomach. I don't think I've ever made her angry. Maybe annoyed when I was a little kid, but not mad. "I need a third party's advice."

"Oh, okay, not what I was expecting, but sure."

"Well, my brother's best friend is here too, Lexi. The – well the only girl in that group over there." I pointed out Lexi with my glass, glad that she was avoiding looking at me.

"How long have they been friends?"

"Um, I don't know, my whole life, maybe. Or at least close."

"Oh, and you've had a crush on her for just as long?" Sarah asked excitedly.

"Something like that." Damn, I could feel my face heating up.

"Nice, now I'm very invested. So what? She's back in town for your brother's wedding?"

"Yeah, and she's staying at my parents' house with me."

"Forced proximity, very good."

"What?"

"Oh, it's a trope in romance novels, you can ignore it. Though if Lexi reads them, you should. Fastest way to figure out what she's into."

"Oh. Um …" Did romance novels go into that stuff? No, not the time to ask. "Anyways, I sorta saw this as an opportunity to get her to, you know, see me as not her best friend's kid brother. And last night, when I picked her up from the bachelorette party, she was super drunk."

"Kaleb, this better end with you tucking her into bed," she said, her voice full of warning.

"It does. But she had asked me to kiss her and … other stuff. And I just told her she could ask for that stuff when she was sober."

"Good boy."

"But either she doesn't remember any of that or she didn't really want it and it was just the alcohol talking. And then when we were – again, this is a bachelor party and I was there for my brother and not –"

"So you were at the strip joint across the street?"

"Yeah." God, how red was I? "This one … worker, took me aside for a dance and Lexi stormed out. I followed her and asked her what was wrong. I figured maybe being the only girl in our group at that kind of place made her uncomfortable. But she just sorta brushed me off, in, like, a passive aggressive way. And when I asked if she was mad at me, she said no. And I just don't know what I did, but it *sucks* having her be mad at me."

"Oh, so like, you're not just crushing on her, you love her, huh?"

"What makes you say that?" I chugged down my drink, suddenly needing as much alcohol inside me as I could get. I hadn't told anyone that I loved her and this girl figured it out after a minute. Was I that obvious?

"Because you pay attention to what she's doing when a stripper is dancing right on you. Pretty sure that's love."

I laughed so hard my beer almost came out my nose. Thank god it didn't, because Lexi looked over just at that moment. She didn't immediately look away this time, so I tried to refocus my attention on Sarah.

"So, here's how I see it. I'm assuming you haven't seen her in a long time, right? So Lexi is probably a little weirded out about how she sees you as an adult now. It'll take time for her to reconcile the two images she has of you and feels comfortable vocalizing her desires. But she is *definitely* attracted to you. And jealous."

"You really think she's jealous?" I asked, maybe a little too hopeful, and she laughed.

"I'm pretty sure given that she's giving me that please-don't-be-hitting-on-him-I-want-him look. Oh and now she's coming over here. Play it cool, Kaleb."

I had downed four drinks since coming here, so playing it cool was not an option. Instead I gestured to the bartender for another drink and didn't turn back around even when Sarah tapped my arm.

"Kaleb?" I didn't mean to turn around so quickly, but as soon as I heard Lexi's voice, and didn't hear the grumbled, angry tone, my heart spun my body around.

"Hey Lex." Yeah, keep it short and sweet, very cool. Beside me, Sarah laughed and Lexi looked at her with a grimace.

"I'm Sarah, nice to meet you," she said, holding out her hand. Lexi smiled politely and shook Sarah's hand before shifting closer to me.

"I'm Lexi, Kaleb's friend."

My friend? Were we friends? Friendly, yeah sure. But friends? That didn't sound right. I sure as hell didn't want to be just her friend.

"Oh, a friend? Cool, cool." Sarah nudged my side, as if she was saying, look at how jealous she is. But I didn't think Lexi looked jealous, just confused and maybe hurt that I was choosing to not go along with the party she'd planned.

"Sorry, Lex, I just needed a break from Jay, you know," I said, offering up the excuse as if that would make things better. Lexi's nose scrunched up at the mention of Jay and she looked over her shoulder, then back to me nodding.

"Yeah, I don't know why he's here. I didn't tell him about the party."

"That's Jay, always showing up uninvited," I murmured and then an awkward silence fell over the three of us. Sarah looked between Lexi and me, both of us distinctly avoiding each other's eyes.

"Well, you've probably gotta go back to your brother. Right, Lexi?" Sarah asked. Lexi met my eyes and then nodded to Sarah. "Family first. Can I see your phone?"

I held the device out, expecting her to make a call or something, but instead she pulled up my contacts and inputted her information. She handed me back my phone with a smile, motioning to Lexi with her eyes. Lexi looked ... kind of pale, her eyes wide in disbelief. And that look only got worse when Sarah got up on her tiptoes, leaned into me, and whispered, "Man up, Kaleb, she wants you to make the first move."

Back on her feet, Sarah smiled at Lexi and me and moved into the crowd and towards the door. Lexi narrowed her eyes at me, then walked away. I followed behind her, not sure if that's what she wanted me to do or not until she spoke.

"So ... are you gonna ask her out?"

"Sarah? No, why?"

"Oh. I was just curious, I guess. Why not?"

"Because ..." I'm in love with you and every girl I've ever gone out with was just a place holder and that wasn't healthy for me or fair to them. If Sarah could read my mind, she'd probably encourage me to say that out loud. But I was scared. Scared that if I confessed any of my feelings for Lexi, she'd tell me she couldn't see me as anything other than her friend's brother. That I wasn't her type. That she only wanted sex.

Sarah reminded me of my deepest hope. Which scared the shit out of me.

CHAPTER 14

Lexi

When I had told Kaleb it was his turn to drink, I didn't think he'd drink this hard. When he came back to the group after talking to that girl, who I shouldn't have any sort of negative feelings for, Kaleb sat next to Jason and drank whatever he was offered by the other man. For most of the night he was quiet, staring off into space in between quick glances my way. But after about 10 drinks, he started getting talkative. Telling jokes, sharing stories, roping strangers into the conversations.

Turns out while I was a horny drunk, Kaleb was a sociable drunk. And I was really glad Sarah wasn't here to see that. Because his socialness extended to an arm around every friend, a big smile for every stranger, and him leaning in far too closely to hear when someone spoke.

When a group of women entered the bar and started eyeing Kaleb, he made it hard to not notice him in the crowd, I placed myself beside him, being a selfish, petulant bitch. But also, if Kat didn't want me using him for sex, I assumed that extended to strangers at bars. And keeping him from drunkenly sleeping with someone was the friendly thing to do. Yeah, my motives were completely friendly and nothing more.

"Lexi!" he cheered as soon as he noticed I was beside him. He wrapped an arm around my shoulder, pulling me into his chest and kissing the top of my head. And the way my heart screamed at the contact, I thought I was going to melt into a puddle. "Are you having fun?"

"Uh, yeah, Kay, I'm having fun." He squinted down at me, brow furrowed and lips turned down. God, was he always this expressive when he drank? I guess I wouldn't know. It's not like he was drinking when I went off to college. I kind of wish I'd come visit with Blake during breaks so that I could see Kaleb and the way he grew into this hunk beside me.

"No, you're not. Why aren't you having fun?"

"I am having fun," I argued, but he wasn't buying it. He leaned into me, hands heading to my stomach and I held my breath. But instead of caressing me or pulling my body into his, he tickled me. This fucking bastard tickled me. And I squealed, loudly, and drew the attention of everyone in the immediate vicinity. Including Blake, who raised an eyebrow at me.

"Is Kay behaving there, Lex?" he asked, eyeing his brother suspiciously. But Kaleb didn't see the warning in Blake's eyes, he was too busy giving me a dopey, crooked smile.

"He's fine, he just tickled me." That softened Blake's expression and he smiled.

"Should I call him a cab?"

"No! I'm good, Lexi's taking me home," Kaleb said, squinting in the direction his brother was but not focusing on him. Blake rolled his eyes and came over to us.

"Lexi, take, like, five steps back," Blake instructed. I did and watched as Blake whispered something into Kaleb's ears. Kay's eyes went wide and he started blushing.

"No, but also, no, that's not -- no," he said, hiding his face behind his hands. Blake chuckled and moved to hug me.

"He's good to go. Though he might not make it up the stairs, so just tuck him in on the couch. Thanks for planning all this, Lex."

"Of course. And I'll take good care of Kaleb." Kaleb smiled when I said his name and shuffled over to hang an arm over my shoulder.

"When did you stop calling him kiddie Kay?" Blake asked, giving me a look.

"I hate that name!" Kaleb groaned, saving me from giving an answer. Blake nodded in response and waved us off, rejoining the rest of the party.

I guided Kaleb out the bar and to his car. When I opened the passenger door, he leaned into me further and took a deep breath.

"You smell real nice, Lex. Is it weird that I wanna use your shampoo so I can smell you on me all the time?"

"I ... I don't know. Ask me again when you're sober." I tried pushing him into the car, but when I'd used his words against him, he stiffened and wouldn't move. When I looked up to meet his eyes, he looked hurt.

"Is that why you're mad at me?" His voice was on the edge of pleading and my breath caught in my throat. I knew he thought I was angry at him, but I didn't think he was hurt by the *idea* that I was mad at him.

"Get in the car, Kaleb," I said quietly.

"Not until you tell me why you're mad. Please. It's killing me."

I looked up at him and those sad eyes that begged for reassurance, reassurance that I wanted to give, but didn't know how without complicating everything else.

"I'm not mad at you, Kay. Honestly. I'm mad at myself. Now please, get in the car." He held my eyes for a moment, then nodded and got in. Once he was buckled, I closed his door and walked over to the driver's side. I took a deep breath before getting in. Kaleb watched as I buckled up and adjusted the seat and mirrors, but he didn't say anything until I was settled in.

"Why're you mad at yourself?"

"Because I – well, I just – I'm irritated at myself for getting irritated about things that don't involve me."

"Is it me?" He shifted in his seat, almost laying on his side, head rested on the head so he could look at me. And it was like he saw through me.

"What? Are you an insightful *and* sociable drunk?" I deflected.

"Yeah, and you're a horny drunk," he said with a laugh, his voice a little high and childish.

"I am not!"

"Yes you are! You wanted me to kiss and touch you *all* over." He'd gone from high pitched to sing song.

"I did not."

"You did too. You just don't remember because you were *drunk* and *horny*."

"Kaleb, if you say the word horny one more time –"

"Horny, horny, horny."

"Oh my god," I groaned and Kaleb laughed, loud and hearty. It was a nice sound, but it settled too quickly and he was quiet, staring at me.

"I'm sorry I made you frustrated. I didn't mean to."

"I know you didn't. This is my issue to solve, not yours."

"It could be though."

"What do you mean?"

He scooted a little closer and reached out to fiddle with my sleeve.

"You could tell me what I did that made you frustrated."

"You didn't do anything wrong, Kaleb."

"When I said that you should ask me when you're sober, I meant that I *wanted* you to ask me when you're sober so I knew it was real. And, you know, I didn't want to take advantage of you when you were drunk. And horny."

"Kaleb."

"And at the strip club, I don't really know what I did wrong, if I was disrespectful or something, but to be honest, I wasn't really looking at the dancer. I just kept thinking about your ass."

"Kaleb!"

"I'm sorry. That's disrespectful too, isn't it?"

"Why were you thinking about my ass?" Now I was laughing. What was this conversation?

"Because you were teasing me last night."

"How exactly was I teasing you?"

"You asked me to massage your legs."

"Uh-huh?"

"You did it cause you knew I wouldn't say no to taking care of you. And then you took off your pants and you moaned."

"I moaned?" Shit, I was worse than I had thought. If I'd acted like that with a lesser man, I would've woken up naked.

"Yeah, and you were doing it on purpose too. That was mean. I couldn't sleep afterwards, my dick hurt so bad." Kaleb was full on pouting now, lip pursed and arms crossed. He was sinking further and further down his seat and when his chin started pulling at his buckle, he pulled himself back up, his motions somehow sharp and fumbling, like only some of his body had gotten the message that he was drunk.

"I'm sorry I teased you." I could barely get the words out without laughing. Kaleb nodded seriously at my apology.

"Will you make it up to me?"

"... how do you want me to do that?" He had just said I made his dick hurt from the teasing. Was he going to ask for some relief? I was very into that. But he was drunk, so no, that was a temptation I'd have to resist.

"Stop being mad at me and yourself, please?"

I looked over to him and he'd pulled out the sweet puppy dog eyes again. And I couldn't say no.

"Okay."

CHAPTER 15

Kaleb

I woke up on the couch, snuggled in three layers of blankets, toast, medicine, and water waiting for me on the coffee table. Slowly, I sat up, my head sensitive to the motion. I downed the food and medicine, then checked my phone.

There was a message from Blake, warning me that if I didn't behave myself, he'd pay to have someone beat me up. Which was … probably smart, I'd wreck his ass. Though I don't know why he bothered sending me that text. He'd made sure all my bravado was wiped out by asking if I was too drunk to get it up before Lexi took me home.

Then there was a message from Sarah, which surprised me. But it just said to keep her updated with my real life romcom, so I guess she just wanted to know how the story ended. The problem was, this wasn't a story. The ending was more likely going to be that I did nothing and she did nothing and we moved on with our lives.

"Oh good, you're up," Mom said as she entered from the kitchen, a half eaten bagel in hand.

"Morning, Mom. Thanks for the toast and stuff." She sat down next to me, her eyes wrinkling as she squinted at the now empty plate.

"Hm, I didn't do that. How was the party last night?"

"Hmm, it was all right. Sorry for crashing on the couch. I'm not messing up your work schedule or anything, right?" Mom patted me on the back sympathetically and shook her head.

"Speaking of the couch, how was it?"

"Fine, I guess, why?" I asked, eyebrow raised.

"Well your Uncle Ray booked his hotel for the wrong date and everywhere else is booked, so ..."

"So I'm sleeping on the couch for the next few days?" I groaned and rested my head back on the couch. This was karma for getting drunk last night and making Lexi take care of my drunk ass. "That's fine. It's only for a few nights, right?"

"Yes, he's only here for the wedding, well and the rehearsal dinner. So three nights total. You sure you're okay with that? Maybe one of your friends can let you crash with them?"

I probably could find someone I to crash with. But then I wouldn't see Lexi in the morning and I'd sleep on the floor for that privilege.

"Nah, it's fine." Mom hugged me from the side and placed a big kiss on my cheek.

"You've turned into such a fine young gentleman, I'm proud of you, Kay."

"Thanks, Mom," I said, hugging her back. She patted my back once more before getting up and continuing her morning work routine.

A little after Mom left, Lexi came down stairs, her steps slow and soft at first, but quickening when she saw I was awake.

"Morning," she said, her voice a little more than a squeak as she bypassed me for the kitchen. I looked down to make sure I hadn't done something weird when I was drunk/asleep like strip down to my birthday suit. But I was full clothed and a quick phone check confirmed that no one had written anything funny on my face.

"Did I do anything weird last night?" I asked, getting up to join her in the kitchen. She was pouring herself a bowl of cereal, which sounded good, so I took out a bowl and grabbed the box once she was finished. When I stepped closer, she gave me a panicked look, her cheeks red.

"No, you didn't do anything. You were ... friendly with everybody, but you didn't do anything weird." Lex looked down at her cereal for a moment, then stepped away from me to sit at the dining room table. I joined her, sitting across from her and eyeing her, as if I'd be able to figure out why she was acting funny just by looking.

I could remember most everything from last night. Or at least the big stuff. The details might've been a little fuzzy, I couldn't remember what we talked about on the car ride home, but I was pretty sure I didn't confess my undying love to her. She would hopefully be acting differently if I had.

"My uncle is gonna be staying in my room tonight until the wedding," I said, mostly just to have something to talk about. "So, you know, make sure you lock the bathroom door to avoid any awkwardness with him."

"Wait, where're you gonna sleep then?" she asked and when I pointed to the couch, she gaped. "No, don't be ridiculous. Have him take Blake's room and I'll sleep on the couch."

"Absolutely not, Lex. No way in hell am I letting you sleep on the couch."

"But Kaleb, it's your --"

"No buts, if you fall asleep on that couch, I will just pick you up and put you in the bed." Shit, maybe that came off too strong, because her face started to get red and she looked away from me, biting her lip. But I was being serious, I wasn't going to let her sleep on the couch.

"Then why don't we just share Blake's bed?" She wasn't looking at me as she said this, which, thank god because I'm sure the panic was written all over my face.

"That's not a good idea, Lex," I managed to choke out.

"Why not?"

Because I was getting hard at just the idea of sharing a bed with you, Lex, geez. How could she ask that? I could feel her gaze come back to me, searching, but I couldn't look up from my cereal.

"We slept together when we were kids. All of us

piled up in the living room with just blankets."

"We're not kids anymore, Lex."

"I know, you're all grown up. Which is why you shouldn't be sleeping on the couch, you're too tall."

"Then I'll sleep on the floor. It's fine, Lex, I promise." I finally met her eyes, trying to convey that I meant every word. And whether she believed me or not, she nodded and dropped the conversation.

❊ ❊ ❊

The literal rehearsals and the rehearsal dinner went by quickly. Probably because I was still thinking about Lexi's offer to share a bed. No amount of grandparents asking why I'm still single or uncles asking if I could look at a mole on their back even after I explain that's not the kind of medicine I study, could distract me from Lexi.

When we practiced walking down the aisle, I was so focused on keeping my eyes on Lexi's head, that when we reached the end, I stumbled over the steps. Then Kat and Blake's tight assed wedding planner gave me a 10 minute long lecture about looking where I was walking. But while I was getting that lecture, Lexi was looking at me, laughing at my misfortune. So on the next run, I tripped again. I'm pretty sure Rachel, the bridesmaid I walked with, was ready to throw me out of the church.

Now, sitting in the Purple Fish for after dinner drinks, I pulled out my phone and opened Sarah's message.

Me: I need your advice again, but if you reference any romcom shit, I'm deleting your number.

Sarah: Ugh, that's a pretty big ask. Can I have, like, a three strike system?

Me: Fine. So one of my family members fucked up their hotel reservations and now they're staying in my room for the rest of the week and I'm taking the couch.

Sarah: One bed trope. Nice.

Me: I don't even know what that means, but I'm assuming that's strike one.

Me: Anyways, when I told Lexi, she tried to offer me her bed. But like, obviously no. And I sorta, kinda said I'd carry her back to bed if she tried to sleep on the couch. Was that bad? Is that too angry macho man?

Sarah: Holy smokes batman! Way to sweep her off her feet (figuratively)!

Sarah: And what you're referring to is an alphahole (alpha man + asshole), which you aren't being. And also, since you brought it up, that shouldn't count as a strike.

Me: Fine, that's fair. But it wasn't too aggressive or anything? She seemed sorta shocked when I said it.

Sarah: She was probably shocked by

how turned on she got by the idea of you manhandling her.

Me: God, I didn't mean I would manhandle her. I just wanted her to know I was serious about her taking the bed.

Sarah: Don't get your panties in a bunch, I said she liked it, didn't I? Keep saying shit like that and she'll drop her panties in a heartbeat.

Me: I don't want her panties off.

Me: Okay, I absolutely do. But I don't want to just have sex.

Sarah: Right, you've loved her for years and if she just used you for sex, you'd be crushed knowing the taste of what you'll never have again.

Me: ...

Me: Shut up.

Sarah: Good things can start with sex. Like children or a bomb ass sexual relationship. Don't be a chickenshit and make a move on her. Tonight. If she offers to sleep on the couch, suggest that you share, but, you know, imply that you won't be doing much sleeping.

Me: ... She actually suggested we sleep together. Like share the bed, not, you know.

Sarah: Kaleb, what the actual fuck?!?!

How could you not bring that up at the beginning? What did you say?

Me: I told her it wasn't a good idea, because it isn't.

Sarah: It is, you're just scared. When she brings it up again, which she will, tell her that if you share a bed, you're not gonna be able to keep your hands to yourself.

Me: That sounds like a threat.

Sarah: No, it's a promise. As long as she still has the option to say no, you're morally good.

Me: Sarah, I can't say that.

Sarah: Yes you can, I believe in you.

"Who're you texting?" Lexi asked, coming up to me from behind and leaning over my shoulder. I quickly locked my phone, praying she didn't see any of Sarah's messages.

"Ah, just a friend. Are you ready to go?" She narrowed her eyes at me, but shook her head, then nodded. We said our goodbyes to the few remaining guests and made our way to the car.

"So are you still planning to sleep on the couch?" she asked as we started to drive off. Was this the moment to use Sarah's line? No, no, she just brought up the couch, not sleeping together. And she probably wouldn't bring it up. I couldn't let Sarah get my hopes up.

"Yeah, that's the plan." Lexi just hummed in response and shifted to look out of the window.

The short drive remained quiet, except for my heart, which pounded in my ears so loudly that I was surprised Lexi didn't notice it. And so that she could continue to not notice, I turned up the radio and sang along to whatever song was playing, hoping that would ease my nerves.

"Kaleb, are you trying to serenade me with One Direction?" Lexi asked, giggling as she curled up in the passenger seat.

"What?" I hadn't been paying attention to what I had been singing along to, the words came to me like a muscle memory, but looking down, the radio read "Last First Kiss - One Direction." Shit, that was on the nose. Did the radio read my mind and try to expose me?

"Oh sorry, I'll change it." I reached for the knob but Lexi's hand interfered, turning the volume up.

"Don't, I like it." And she started singing along at full volume, slightly out of tune and gravely, but beautiful. Shit, I'd listen to her sing for hours. But I didn't have the chance, because we arrived at home and I had no excuse for staying in the car to listen to music with her.

Lexi hummed as we walked into the house and I opened the door to an already made couch, blankets and pillows laid out. Mom had even grabbed my charger from my room and hooked it up. I took a deep breath and sat down on the couch, surprised when Lexi plopped down beside me.

"Are you not going to bed yet?" I asked.

"Are you really gonna sleep here?" She looked

around at the couch, face scrunched up.

"Yes." I swallowed, finding it hard to pull my eyes away from the lip she was chewing on.

"Are you sure you don't wanna share the bed with me?"

Fuck.

"Lex, I can't share a bed with you." Sarah was right, I'm a chicken.

"Why not?" Lexi looked up to me, eyes questioning. And that question pushed me over the edge.

"Because if I get into bed with you, I don't think I have the willpower to keep my hands to myself." I put my head in my hands and rested my elbows on my knees and waited. Waited for her to say that I was being gross or that she was disappointed in me or say that she still saw me as a kid.

But none of that happened. Instead she pulled one arm away so I was forced to look at her. She'd shifted so that she was facing me, sitting on her legs. She rubbed my arm, her thumb drawing little circles that sent goosebumps up my arms. She shifted again, leaning forward, eyes drifting closed, and bringing our lips together. It was a quick kiss, just enough to feel the pressure of her. But god, it was the best feeling ever.

"Come to bed with me, Kaleb."

CHAPTER 16

Lexi

"**A**re you sure?" Kaleb asked after I kissed him and invited him into my bed. If some other guy had said that after I kissed them, I would've been self conscious, worried that they didn't want what I had to offer. But that wasn't Kaleb. Kaleb was licking his lips like he was trying to memorize the taste of me in case I did say I was mistaken. And his eyes, fuck, he was looking me over like he was trying to decide what he wanted to do first.

"I'm sure. I'm very sure." He grunted in reply, like his words weren't something he was capable of anymore. Then his other hand, because I was still holding onto his arm, moved to cup my cheek. His thumb stroked me gently before he brought my face to his. The pressure of his lips felt so good, I leaned further into him and he opened his mouth in response, his tongue grazing my lips till I gave way.

At first, his tongue was slow and tender, but when I moaned at the pleasure of him and his movements became hungry. His hands dropped to my waist and he dragged me onto his lap, pulling me close so that my hot need rested against his. I rocked against him once and his grip on my waist tightened, holding me in place.

"Lex, I've wanted to kiss you for so fucking long. If you do that one more time, I'm gonna cream my pants. Please, please don't make me embarrass myself like that." I whined, trying to push against him again but his grip held firm. He chuckled at my desperation, resting his head on my shoulder. "Do you really want me that bad, Lex? Or is this just a dream? You didn't have anything to drink, did you?"

"It's real and I'm completely sober," I whispered, reaching up to run my fingers through his hair and leaving gentle kisses on his neck, making him groan. He stood up, holding me close so that I slid down his body and landed on my feet. He kissed the top of my head, holding me flesh against his body. We stood there for a minute, relishing the moment as Kaleb stroked my hair. Or maybe he was relishing the moment, because all I could think about was how hard he was pressed against me, long and thick and making me restless with need.

When he finally let go of me, he turned to the couch and started futzing with the blankets there.

"What're you doing?" I asked, my voice pitched high in annoyance. My body was ready for him. That one kiss was enough to get me wet and I didn't want any further delay.

"I'm trying to make it look like I slept here. If I get

so lost in your body and forget, do you wanna be the one to explain to my mom where I slept?" he asked, a smile pulling his lips up when I groaned in reply. He was being smart, of course he was, but I didn't want smart right now. I wanted him.

When the blankets were crumbled to his satisfaction, he turned and kissed me, hard. His hands held my head, angling me gently so that his tongue could tangle onto mine. He was warm and just the right amount of forceful. And just when I was going to beg for him to move me to the bed or the couch or wherever the fuck he wanted, he scooped me up. One arm under my legs and the other behind my back, carrying me up the stairs as he buried his face in my neck, grazing his tongue over the soft skin.

"You've gotta be quiet, Lex," he whispered into my ear, his breath sending chills down my spine. And I must've made some sort of noise, because Kaleb chuckled again. He quickened his pace to the bedroom and we winced when the stairs squeaked underneath us. But when the door finally closed behind us, I felt unleashed. Kaleb set me on the bed and my legs instantly wrapped around him, pulling his hips to mine. Our lips were back together and I grazed his bottom lip with my teeth, making him groan. And god that sound, I wanted more of it. To know that I was pleasing him, making him lose control.

"Lex, I can't fuck you here."

Panic swarmed my mind and I felt my heavy breathing halt.

"Why not?"

"Well, for one, this is my brother's bed." Oh, he just meant here. My heart settled down and I pulled him closer so that his cock rocked against me.

"It's okay. I jerked off here just the other day."

"You did?" His voice came out choked, his eyes rolling to the back of his head as I rocked against him again.

"Yeah. After you pinned me to the wall at the bar, I was … really hot and bothered."

"Is that what you like, baby?"

"Mhmm." Kaleb grabbed my hands, pinning them over my head as he leaned further into me, his weight like a blanket covering me, keeping me safe and warm. And god, yes, that was really doing it for me.

"I wanna know every single thing that gets you going so I can please you. But …" He thrusted against me, hard, the bed squeaking underneath us and a small moan leaking from my lips. "I can't do that for you here, not with the way you moan. So we're going to climb out the window and fuck in the treehouse."

"What? Is that where you take all your girls?" I laughed, but the question was a leaked insecurity that I wish I could take back. Kaleb froze on top of me, letting my hands go so that he could caress my face.

"I won't lie to you, Lex, I've made out with some girls in there. But I like to think I'm considerate, so I never tried to fuck in there. With you, I can't wait, I wanna be inside you so bad, I don't care if it's a little uncomfortable. Is that okay with you?"

"Fuck yes."

Kaleb pulled me up, standing so that our bodies

were flushed together again. He took a deep breath, then took my hand and led me to the window. Once open, Kaleb stepped out of the window and held his hand out. After he helped me climb through the window, we tiptoed across the roof to the treehouse, which had a patio like area that was just one step from the roof. Why had I never noticed the treehouse was so close? Maybe because Kaleb was the one who helped his dad build it, so Blake never really used it.

Once inside, I realized Kaleb wasn't exaggerating when he said it wouldn't be comfortable. The house was maybe an inch or two taller and deeper than Kaleb was tall and the wooden floor was only partially covered by a well worn rug. But the door and windows were covered with red fabric, and right now, that was all I needed to be comfortable jumping this sweet, tender, sexy man. So as soon as we stepped in, I stood on my tip toes, wrapped my arms around his neck, and pulled him into a kiss. He groaned into me, walking me backward into the wall and pinning me there with his body. He pushed against me once, so I could get of full feel of him, and then he backed away,

"Kaleb," I whined, but then I felt his hands cup against my breasts, kneading me and making me moan.

"I thought you didn't care about breasts," I murmured and Kaleb let out one dry laugh.

"I said I didn't care about *that* woman's breasts. I never said anything about how I felt about *your* breasts."

"And how do you feel?"

"Let me show you." His fingers dropped down to the hem of my shirt and pulled it over my head, tossing it to the corner of the treehouse. His fingers slowly drifted up my ribs, occasionally stopping to massage an area, and his eyes smiled each time I moaned at his touch. When he reached the edge of my sports bra, he slipped his fingers in, but didn't go further than the underside of my breasts.

"On or off, baby? Which will get you hotter?"

"Off, god, take it off, please. I want you to touch me more." God the way he asked just made me wetter and wetter. And it didn't sound like he was asking to know what to do. He was asking because he'd thought of hundreds of ways to take me and he wanted me to pick which one.

With a grunt, he pulled my sports bra up and over my head. And his breath hitched as he looked down on me, hands beginning to knead my breasts again, his thumb just grazing over my nipples. And he was right, we couldn't have done this in Blake's room, because I was a whining mess. I whimpered each time his thumb brushed my nipple and groaned when Kaleb leaned in to kiss my neck.

His lips fell away from my neck, drifting further down until he was kissing my nipple, keeping a steady rhythm as he kneaded the other. He switched to my other breast, his kisses turning into quick sucks. Then back to the other to do the same and adding flicks of his tongue.

"Kaleb," I breathed, not able to vocalize the need. I felt on the edge, like one more nudge in the right direction would push me over. Kaleb nodded, shifting so that his knee pushed between my legs, putting a wonderful pressure against me. Without thinking, I rocked against him, heat rising and rising. Kaleb's free hand went to my waist and guided me into a quicker pace.

"Kaleb."

"You're getting there, aren't you, baby?"

"This isn't fair," I murmured, the words hard to get out as the pleasure bubbled up inside me.

"How so?" His breath tickled the sensitive tips of my nipples and when my body shivered in response, he kissed me gently before continuing his sucking and teasing.

"You wouldn't let me make you come in your pants."

"I'm sorry, baby, but let me be selfish on this one point. Let me watch you come as many times as you can before I get off. Okay?"

Shit, that was hot. Had I ever been with someone who actively wanted me to come first? And not just come first, but multiple times before them. When Kaleb said he wanted to please me, he fucking meant it. And that was what pushed me to an orgasm. That and the way he rubbed his leg on my clit and how he started sucking my nipples loudly.

"Kaleb," I moaned, my body burning. He kissed my nipple one last time before pulling away, his hands going to my lower back and his fingers rubbing in gentle circles.

"Do you need some cool down time?" he asked

and I nodded, unable to catch my breath. He stood back up, leaning his chest against me, but distinctly holding his hips away.

"Is it bad that I wanna keep teasing your body?" he asked, kissing my cheek.

"Do you want me to melt?"

"A little." Kaleb knelt down, kissing a line down the center of me, mercifully leaving my breasts alone, and stopping at the hem of my jeans.

"Are you ready for me to take these off? I wanna see how wet I made you." I couldn't do anything but nod, my stomach hollowing in response to his tickling breath. He undid the button and zipper before pulling everything down. I held onto his shoulder as I stepped out of the clothes. He tossed them away like they'd offended him, like anything that kept me from him was a crime.

He shifted my legs open wider, propping my back against the wall and taking me in, licking his lips as he did. He massaged my thighs, one hand on each, making a slow trail up to my center. The anticipation alone was making me shake.

"Do you need more time?" he asked, moving closer to me to kiss my thigh, his stubble tickling me.

"No. Touch me. Please."

"Oh baby, I'm gonna do more than that."

And instead of bringing his fingers up to my sex, his hands grabbed my ass and pulled me forward to his mouth. I gasped, my hands going to his shoulders and digging in. He licked all the way up me once and moaned, the sound vibrating through my body.

"God Lex," he murmured before using his tongue to slide around my lips, making long circles around my opening. I pushed my hips into him, groaning, and I could feel him smile against me. One hand left my ass and came between my thighs as his tongue moved its focus to my clit. He pressed the flat of his tongue against me, moving around in tiny circles, while one finger slid inside me, curling to hit the spot that made me cry out his name. He quickened the pace of his tongue as he stroked my g-spot, sliding in another finger when I moaned out again.

"Kaleb, please."

"Please what, baby?" The second he was done speaking, his mouth closed around my clit and sucked, matching the pace of his fingers thrusting into me.

"I want you inside me, please. I wanna make you feel good too." Those words didn't seem enough to describe my desire to please him. He made my body feel on fire. I wanted to feel proof that I did the same to him.

Kaleb froze for a few seconds, then pulled back to kiss my thighs, slowing the pace of his fingers, but not stopping.

"Sorry, baby, no can do. I don't have a condom. But don't worry, I'm getting off just fine. Relax and let me eat you up." His mouth returned to my sex, his free hand moving from my ass to his jeans, undoing them so he could stroke himself in his boxers. And that small glimpse of his cock made my body shake with need.

"Is that one of the things that gets you off, baby? Watching me stroke myself because I can't get in you?"

"Kaleb," I whined. "You said we were gonna fuck. You said you wanted inside me. I want you inside me. I *need* you."

"I know, I know, I'm sorry. I do want to be in you. Your pussy is squeezing so tight on my fingers right now, you're making it so *hard* to do the right thing. I wasn't thinking straight when I brought you here."

"Kaleb, please, as long as you're, you know, I don't mind if it's bare. It actually sounds *real good*. Please."

"I'm good, baby, but if I stick it in you bare, 1) I won't last long and I get the feeling coming inside of you once will be the end of me, I won't want to do anything else ever again, and 2) I don't want to go to CVS afterwards. I want to get you into bed, massage you all over, and hold you in my arms as you fall asleep."

"I'm on the pill, so I don't need anything else." God, I would say anything to get his dick inside me.

"Mhmm, and have you been taking that pill regularly this week?"

Shit, no, I haven't. I'd been drunk or distracted by him.

"Then just pull out before you come."

"Baby, that's easier said than done and I haven't … done it before. Are you gonna listen to me when I tell you to slow down?" I nodded my head eagerly, even though I wasn't sure I could keep that promise. He'd stopped sucking my clit, but his fingers kept thrusting inside of me, slow so as to keep me right on edge.

"And you're sure this is what you want?"

"Yes, god, Kaleb, please. Put your dick inside me before I combust."

"Well we wouldn't want that," he said through a chuckle. He pulled his fingers out of me and stuck them in his mouth, keeping eye contact with me as my knees started to buckle and I slid down the wall.

Kaleb stood, pulling me back to my feet and kissing me while he tugged his pants and boxers all the way down, kicking them to the side. My hands went to the hem of his shirt, tugging it up so I could feel the heat of his skin against mine. Once his clothes were gone, his lips left mine and he laid down on the floor, gesturing for me to get on top of him.

"I'm sorry you don't get to pick, baby, but this is probably the most comfortable position for you. So ride me."

I didn't hesitate. I straddled over him, took hold of his cock, and slid it inside me, letting my hips fall into him.

"Lexi, fuck," Kaleb moaned, his hands taking hold of my waist to stop my slow circles. "I said slow, remember? You can't just put me in balls deep like that."

I didn't say anything, but grumbled, my hips rocking on their own. Kaleb's body shuddered under me. And that felt *so good*. But I wanted to make him feel better and the one thing I knew about Kaleb's pleasure was that it was tied to mine. So I kept still for a moment, fighting the overwhelming need inside me until his grip on my waist loosened. Then I took one of his hands to my clit and the other to one of my nipples, and he eagerly worked to please.

"God, Lex, I love that. Please, show me what you like, I wanna know it all. I wanna fulfill your every single desire."

He rubbed and pinched me, sending large shivers through my body. I started to bounce on his cock, making him moan each time he slid deep inside me. His hips started to move, matching my rhythm, his eyes rolling to the back of his head. I'd never been on top like this before and the control I had on his pleasure, made me think I might never choose another position again.

"You gotta slow down, baby."

But I didn't want to. I wanted to go faster, feel him come inside me while I came. Because I was just as close as he was, just a few more hard strokes would get us there.

"Lex," Kaleb warned, his hands going to grip my ass just as I slammed down onto him and felt him fill me while I convulsed over the edge. Still shaking and out of breath, I laid down on his chest and his hands moved to hug me to him.

"Lex, did you do that on purpose?"

"Not really, I just … wanted to feel you. So … maybe a little."

"You're lucky I like you."

"I like you too." I felt Kaleb's chest pause beneath me for a moment. When I lifted my head to look at him, he was smiling softly, one hand coming up to rest my head against him and stroke my hair.

CHAPTER 17

Kaleb

The CVS was too bright for 2:00 in the morning. Soft saxophones played in the background while we waited in line behind a loud, older woman asking about her creme.

"Are you happy with yourself?" I asked Lexi, more than a little grumpy that we were here instead of snuggled up in bed. But Lexi didn't seem bothered by it at all. Rather she seemed happy, a small smile coming to her face whenever she wasn't saying something. And the idea that I did that was more than enough to forgive her for causing this late night trip. I mean, I was to blame too. I could see the desire on her face, could feel her quickening pace, and I didn't stop her until it was too late. I wanted to blame it on the fact that I'd never had sex without a condom. But to be honest, I wanted to come inside her just as much as she wanted me to.

"I am, actually." Her voice was a little sing-song, as she trailed her hand over the boxes and bottles in the aisle. I rolled my eyes, but I couldn't help but smile. How could I not be happy? The love of my life just gave me the best sex of my life. *And* she told me she liked me. I was in heaven.

"Good." I caught her arm and pulled her into a hug, kissing the top of her head. And god it felt good to be able to do that, just kiss her when I want, hold her. There was no coming back from this, I was a goner. If I screwed this up, I'd probably become a hermit.

In front of us, the old lady left and the pharmacist waved us forward. I stepped up to the counter and Lex disappeared behind one of the aisles.

"Lex," I called, but she didn't reemerge or say anything. I sighed and looked to the pharmacist, a tired man about my age, maybe slightly older. "Can I get a box of whatever the most effective emergency contraceptive is?"

The man nodded, moving to the shelves behind him to grab a box, then returned to scan it. "Will that be all?"

"And this," Lexi said, popping up behind me and setting a very large box of condoms on the counter. A variety pack. With over 100 condoms.

"Did you just grab the biggest box they had?"

"Yup, you were good, I want more," she whispered, holding onto my arm as she stood on tiptoes to reach my ear. God, she did that on purpose, didn't she?

"I have condoms at home."

"But not where we need them."

"Fine," I grumbled, then to the pharmacist, "We'll

also take the oversized box of condoms."

The man nodded, scanned it, and gestured to the card reader. I paid the absurd amount and we gathered our goods. Lex held the box of condoms, half skipping as we left. I opened up the medicine and began reading through the small printed list of directions and side effects.

"Are you sure you're okay taking this?" I asked, squinting to read.

"Yup, give it here." She took the box and pulled out a single pill, popping it in her mouth and swallowing without water.

"Wait, was there only one pill in there? And you should take pills with water."

"Yup," she said, completely ignoring my other point.

"That was one damn expensive pill that seems just as likely to cause blood clots as to prevent pregnancy." Lexi took the paper from me, balling it up and throwing it away in the trash just outside the store.

"I can't believe you're actually reading that," she laughed.

"Have you not read it?"

"No, no one does. You're just a big nerd."

"I don't think it's nerdy to be concerned about your health."

"You're right, it's sweet." She kissed my cheek and ran to the car, letting herself in. When I joined her inside, she'd opened the condom box and was shoving two of each kind into the glove box.

"Do you plan on hiding condoms in every corner of my life?"

"Yes. And don't buckle up." My fingers halted on the seat belt and I squinted at Lexi as she put the box down and leaned in to kiss me. There was no more hesitation in her kisses. She pursed her lips against mine, then parted, tongue eagerly meeting mine.

"What're you doing, Lexi?" I asked, because her hand reached down to my crotch, scooping my balls and pulling her hand up my shaft.

"You made me come more than once, it's my turn."

"Lex, I'm a little sensitive right now and we're in a parking lot," I breathed against her lips. But I couldn't bring myself to stop her as she undid my pants and pulled me out. She stroked my full length slowly, pausing at my tip to run her thumb over it.

"It's late, there's no one here to see us." She pulled away from my lips and gathered her hair up as she leaned down.

"You don't have to do this, baby. I got off making you come, it's not something you owe me for."

"I know," she said, her breath tickling my cock and making it twitch. "But the feeling is mutual, so let me do this."

She kissed the head gently, breathing me in. A series of insecurities flood my mind, only to be dashed away the second her lips tongue slid over my head. She went painfully slow, her tongue caressing every bit of me. Her hand continued pumping as she slid me into her mouth, the movements quickening as she took me further.

"Fuck, baby." I couldn't keep my eyes open as she started bobbing her head. One of my hands went to the seat, clutching it till my fingers went white as I tried to resist the urge to thrust into her. My other hand went to her hair, taking over holding it for her. With her now free hand, she cupped my balls, gently rolling them in her palm. Heat swelled up inside me, increasing as she sucked my head then plunged me deep into her throat.

"Don't push yourself, baby." She looked up at me and winked, pulling her head up and wrapping her tongue around my tip, making little circles over and over.

"I'm gonna come soon, baby." Lexi smiled against me, then bobbed her head down, sucking as much of me as she could manage. She'd push herself a little further and I could feel her throat contract against me. I tugged as gently as possible on her hair to pull her up, but she didn't want to go. "Baby, I'm gonna come, please."

In response to this, she stroked me faster, her mouth focusing on sucking my tip. Her hand left my balls to gently pat my thigh, a sign that she wanted it. And despite my better judgment, I gave it to her with a loud grunt that echoed in the car.

When she sat up, I immediately reached for the glove box to grab napkins. Then reached to the back of the car where I had a pack of water bottles. I held out the items to her, but she only took the water.

"Are you not gonna spit it out?" I asked. She

smiled and stuck her tongue out at me, my come noticeable missing.

"Thanks for the treat." She winked as she took big gulps of water.

"Shit, I'm sorry. We can go to McDonald's or something, get you some soda, something to cover the taste."

"Kaleb, you shot right to the back of my throat, I didn't get the chance to taste it. A shame, really." She capped the water and set it aside, then leaned in to kiss my cheek and pull my pants back up.

"So you just like driving me crazy and not listening, huh?" I zipped and buttoned my pants, then buckled up, looking around to make sure no one was in the parking lot. It was thankfully empty.

"Kaleb, the past few days I've been fighting a massive lady boner over you. I'm done fighting. Plus, in case you didn't know, you also deserve several orgasms. And I'm more than happy to be the one giving them to you."

"God, what am I gonna do with you, Lex?"

"I dunno, fall in love with me, maybe?"

CHAPTER 18

Lexi

I woke up in Blake's room, in Kaleb's arms, and I felt wholly contented. I'd said something rather foolhardy last night, telling him he should fall in love with me, high on the endorphins of sex, but it didn't scare him off. Instead he just smiled like he knew something I didn't and kissed my cheek.

Shit, I was getting it bad. Not only had the sex been amazing and the after care sweet and tender, he seemed to genuinely not want to let me go. The guys I'd had sex with before, if we weren't immediately going to bed afterwards, would create space between us, because they were hot or sweaty or they just weren't into snuggling. And yeah, you could argue they were just dicks, they absolutely were and I was fine with it at the time because I was ultimately just in it for the sex, but Kaleb's sweetness didn't seem like the standard either. He didn't just make sure I was all right and didn't have any regrets, he bought extra protection, went along with my big condom box gag, and fed me. Then when we were finally heading to bed, he didn't let me fall asleep in my contacts and he helped me change when tiredness started to overwhelm me.

I shifted in Kaleb's arms to look up at him. He'd been awake, texting someone, but when he saw that I was awake, he set the phone aside and kissed my forehead.

"What're your opinions on good morning kisses?" he asked, voice gravelly and that did things for me. I wrapped my leg around his waist and pulled him closer. He smiled, one hand coming up to cup my cheek and kissed me. Our tongues reached for each other, not hungry but just with the need to touch and feel the other's warmth.

"I like morning kisses," I murmured when we parted. He smiled, but a flash of his phone caught in his eye and he moved his hand away from me.

"Who're you texting so early?" I tightened my leg around him, feeling a little territorial. I wanted this moment to be just us.

"Sorry, I was just texting Sarah about … stuff before you woke up." A small blush crept over his cheeks and I felt my body stiffen. Sarah was the girl from the bar the other day, right? And he was texting her while in bed with me after the night we had? No, I need to cool down. We didn't talk about what we were doing, if we were dating or if this was just sex. And we certainly didn't talk about exclusivity. I didn't have the right to be upset. But damn, it scared me that he was texting her right now.

I let my leg fall off him and was about to turn to get up, but Kaleb pulled me back to him and tossed his phone to the side.

"Sorry, Lex, I didn't do that right. Forgive me? It's just a little embarrassing."

"What?" Had my insecurities been that easy to read?

"Um yeah. Sarah, she's the one we met at the bar the day before yesterday. There was some dude creeping on her at the bar, so I just sorta got in the way. And she thanked me and said she owed me one. And normally I wouldn't've asked for anything, but you were mad at me for the whole strip club thing, so I asked for her advice."

"Advice? On me?"

"Yeah. She really likes romance novels, so she's sorta invested in our story. Apparently brother's best friend is a common trope. I can show you the texts, if that'll make you feel more comfortable. It's just, you can't look at me while you're reading them, okay? It's embarrassing."

Wow, Kaleb really was something. I don't think Blake would've told him about the men who'd cheated on me, but even if he had, Kaleb's response felt natural. Like even if he hadn't known, he'd have been able to pick out the panic in my response.

"I don't need to see your phone, I trust you." Kaleb let out a sigh of relief, making me laugh.

"Sorry, I'm just glad you don't have to see me so embarrassed so early on." Early on in what? Was this a relationship or a fling? I was too scared to ask because I wasn't sure what answer I wanted. Normally I'd ask Kat for advice, but, god bless her, she wouldn't be able to keep it a secret like this from Blake. It was too big and that man knew how to read her and she'd crack like a pinata. My jealousy towards Sarah turned into jealousy of having someone like Sarah, someone uninvolved. All my friends I was close enough to talk to about something like this were mutual friends with Kat or Blake.

"Do you read romance novels? Like the ... explicit ones?" Kaleb asked, looking up and biting his lip.

"Explicit? What you mean like romance books with murder?"

"No, like with ... sex." Kaleb's ears were reddening and god, he was so cute.

"No, I've not read any of those. Why?" I asked through a giggle, scooting closer so I was even with his face.

"Well I was gonna say I wanted to read your favorites. But we could read them together too. If you're interested, that is."

I took hold of his face, angling him down so he'd look at me. Kaleb seemed to relax, his breathing evening out as I held him there. I kissed his forehead, the tip of his nose, each of his cheeks, then his lips, savoring the taste of him.

"Did you have plans for today?" he asked.

"No, but I do now." I slid my hands down his chest then up his shirt, humming with pleasure at the feel of his warm, hard muscles.

"Lex?" he said, his voice a little strained.

"Hmm?" I let my hands continue their upward ascent, stopping only when I reached his pecs and could feel his pounding heart.

"Let's go out. On a date."

"A date?" I repeated. That word surprised me. He could've asked me to go hang out, grab a bite with him, but the word date was direct and came with implications. Date meant that this wasn't just sex, right?

"Yes, a proper date. We can do *this* later." He took hold of my hands through his shirt and pressed them there, his heartbeat and breath quickening against my touch.

"Promise?" The effect I was having on his body started being mirrored in my own, a warm need flooding through me.

"Promise," he said with a kiss.

* * *

I don't know what kind of date I expected from Kaleb, but this wasn't it. He'd picked out my clothes, breathable leggings and a loose tank top, and packed a bag of spare clothes, towels, and soaps. So I half expected him to take me on some day trip in the woods where we'd stay in a cabin and fuck all day.

But instead we were at a sort of gym. Except gym wasn't the right word to describe it. There were several sections of ... activities, I guess. There was a rock wall, a section of floor that was just trampolines and another section that was a foam pit, and above us people were balancing on beams. And maybe most importantly, there were children running wild through the building, exhausted adults yelling at them from the sides of the attractions.

"Sorry, I didn't think there'd be that many people here since it's a weekday. Do you wanna go somewhere else?" Kaleb asked, a hand raking through his curls and his brow furrowing. He was cute when he was flustered. I took his hand, giving him a little squeeze before walking to the counter.

"Hey, Kay, whatcha doing here?" the man at the counter asked. He looked about Kaleb's age and was slightly familiar, though I couldn't place where I recognized him from.

"Hey Russ, just out on a mid day date. Don't tell your brother though, I don't need him acting like an ass at the wedding," Kaleb said, pulling out his wallet.

"Brother?" I repeated, reaching to grab his card before he could put it in the reader. He raised his brow at me. "You paid for my drinks earlier this week and for … stuff last night. Let me get this."

"Nope, not happening. And this is Jason's brother, his family owns the place."

"Oh."

"Yeah, that's the effect Jay has on people. But don't worry, Kay, I won't say anything. I know how much of an ass he can be," Russ said, sighing a little at the thought of his big brother. While I was looking at Russ, with a newfound sympathy for all of Jason's relatives, Kaleb snuck his card into the reader and paid for our passes.

"Sign these and you're good to go. Those kids're here for a field trip, but they should be leaving in 30 minutes or so." Russ handed us liability waivers and once we signed them, gestured for us to head into the main area. Kaleb took my hand, walking me over to a cubby to store our things, then to the center of the room.

"So, what do you wanna do first? Oh wait." Kaleb knelt down, drawing the attention of every adult in the room until his hands went for my shoes, retying the loose knots. God, I understood the strangers expecting something since they didn't know we just got ... together, but why did my heart stop too? Maybe I just had marriage on the brain because of Kat and Blake.

"Mister, mister, me too, please!" a kid shouted, shoelaces flopping as she ran up to Kaleb. Kaleb laughed and, when he finished tying my shoes, moved to tie the little kid's. The girl gave Kaleb a big smile, said thank you, and ran off. But just as Kaleb started to stand up, another kid came up with untied shoes. And then another and another. And Kaleb tied their shoes without a word of complaint.

"You're good with kids, huh?" I asked when he finally was able to stand without a child approaching him.

"I dunno if I'd say good. I just tied their shoes." He shrugged and took my hand, leading us over to the rock climbing wall, where there were fewer kids.

"It's kinda sexy though," I whispered into his ear and he raised an eyebrow at me, eyes starting to darken.

"Lex, don't tell me things like that or else I'm gonna spend the whole time looking for untied shoes."

We stepped up to the rock climbing wall and Kaleb waved away the employee there and grabbed the harnesses himself. He knelt down again and held out the harness for me. I stepped in and he pulled the harness up, his fingers grazing all the way up my legs. If he'd noticed the way my body reacted to his touch, he didn't show it and focused on securing and tightening the straps.

Once Kaleb got his own harness on, we stood in line for the ropes, employees at the front of the line, watching as kids climbed to the top and then ricocheted back to the ground. The boy in front of us wiggled nervously, bouncing back and forth on his feet as he watched his friends.

"Hey kid, turn around," Kaleb instructed, kneeling down as the kid turned to face him. Kaleb started readjusting the kid's harness, moving it so it wasn't cutting into the kid's neck. "You nervous?"

"Um, no," the kid lied.

"Yeah? Well I am." Kaleb cupped a hand around his mouth and loudly whispered, "But I'm trying to look cool for the girl I'm with, so don't tell her, okay?"

The kid giggled and looked up to me with a big smile before turning back to Kaleb.

"I won't, mister."

"Thanks. Now, I want you to know, you don't have to climb the wall if you don't want to. And you don't have to go all the way to the top either. Do whatever makes you comfortable, okay?" Kaleb waited for the kid to nod, then added, "And don't fiddle with your harness too much, okay? The straps need to stay like this to keep you safe."

The kid nodded and turned when the employee called for the next person. Kaleb stood back up and I leaned into him, snuggling up into the crook of his shoulder.

"You're doing it again," I whispered, reaching behind to grab his ass. Kaleb grunted, and put his arm under mine, pulling my hand up his back and letting his hand rest on the small of my back.

"Are you always this ... eager?" he asked, pulling me close to kiss the top of my head.

"No, it's all for you baby," I said, surprising myself with how honest the words were. "Now go climb that wall before I climb you."

* * *

After several different activities that required more balance than I possessed and a quick shower, we were seated at the fanciest hipster restaurant I had ever been to. There was odd, abstract art and statues everywhere and the wall that wasn't covered in art was either exposed brick or shiplap.

"Is this the kind of place you usually go to?" I asked, eyeing the three foot piggy bank statue behind Kaleb.

"No, but I wanted to take you somewhere nice

that wasn't crazy fancy. So, hipster farm to table restaurant it is. Don't order the sweet tea though, they use agave instead of sugar."

"Agave? Is that just like a bad substitute?"

"Um, yeah, it's not … well it can upset your stomach." Kaleb blushed a little and I laughed.

"I wanna make a dirty joke out of that, but I can't think of anything."

"Probably for the best," he grumbled. "Are you excited for tomorrow?"

"For the wedding? Or seeing you in a suit? Because yes to both."

"You're cute. How's your speech going?"

Shit, I slammed my head into my hands and groaned.

"That good, huh?"

"I got distracted," I grumbled and Kaleb furrowed his brow.

"By what?"

"You, dumbass." I nudged his leg with my foot, making him laugh.

"Sorry, I'll leave you alone for the rest of the day, if you want."

"No, I very much do not want that. You made promises. I'll just write it while we eat."

"How about you talk about the time he ate, like, a bucket full of dirt?"

"Oh my god, I'd forgotten about that! Why the hell was he eating dirt for?"

"I think Jason dared him too."

"Is Jason the center of all our worst stories? I went

to a party with him and Blake once and the second I stepped through the door, this dude threw up all over me." We laughed but then our waitress cleared her throat beside us. "Sorry."

"It happens all the time … unfortunately. Y'all ready to order?"

Food and drinks ordered, Kaleb listed off several embarrassing stories about Blake, each of which I jotted down in my phone. Because while I knew most of the stories and had been there when they'd happen, Kaleb knew about the aftermath. And apparently their mother had a sense of irony. Blake snuck extra dessert when he was supposed to be in bed, his mom made him eat a big bowl of chocolate pudding. Blake and Kaleb snuck out to go to a movie, they had to watch three horror films before bed.

And then a text ruined my mood.

"What's up?" Kaleb asked.

"Oh, a … an ex texted me. He heard I was in town and wanted to meet up." I set the phone face down on the table, not wanting to look at it. The man in question had been my first everything, minus the kiss between Blake and me, but I was not the first of anything for him. It was stupid. I was very much into Kaleb right now. I didn't miss the man or want anything to do with him ever again. But his message reminded me of what it's like to be dropped like a hot potato. And I still wasn't certain about how Kaleb felt, still too afraid to ask and hear this was just a fling for him, that I was just one of the many girls who he wouldn't actually fall for.

"Can I see?" Kaleb asked, gesturing for the phone. I don't know why I did it, but I nodded and Kaleb took the phone, eyes narrowing at the message.

"Lex?"

"Mhmm?

"Can I text this man and then block his number?" I looked up to meet Kaleb's eyes, thrown off by the aggression there. He looked like he wanted to crush my phone in his fist.

"What're you gonna text him?"

"That you're too busy getting railed by a real man to meet up with him."

"Kaleb!"

"I'm doing it." I reached over the table to grab my phone, but Kaleb took advantage of his long limbs to play keep away as he texted. "Sent."

"Kaleb, I swear," I muttered.

"What? Did you want to meet up with him?"

"No." I answered quickly and I hope Kaleb didn't see it as me being eager to keep things going with him, even though that's totally what it was. "I just figure it'd be best to not engage in any conversation."

My phone flashed in his hand and Kaleb looked down at it, eyebrow raised.

"That was a fast reply," he murmured, tapping my phone to open the message. "He says congrats. With a period. I'm still gonna block him."

"Why're you doing this, Kay?"

"Because I saw your face when you saw his message. No one's gonna make you look like that if I can help it." He handed me back my phone and I shoved it in my pocket, trying not to dwell on his words and the meanings I wanted to read into.

"Thanks," I murmured, just as the waitress set the check down on the table, a gentle nudge for us to get out after verging on two hours of being here.

"Let me pay for this, please," I said, snatching the bill before he had a chance.

"Do you normally argue to pay on dates? Or is it because you still kind of see me as a kid?"

Is that what I was doing? He had a point, I didn't put up any fight to pay on other dates, so why was it important that pay now? But he had spent at least a couple hundred on me already. And it didn't feel right to let him do that when he was still a student. Was that me treating him as a kid?

Kaleb slid the check out of my hands while I was thinking, waving to the waitress, who came and took his card.

"Lex, we're gonna go back home and I'm gonna make sure you can never see me as a kid again. And I'm sure as hell gonna make you forget about that asshole. Okay?"

CHAPTER 19

Kaleb

When we got back to my house, it was empty. But with the way my anxiety mixed with desire, I wanted to make sure we wouldn't get caught or interrupted. So I scooped her up and carried her into the bathroom. Inside, with the door locked, I set her on the counter, pulling her forward so I could stand between her legs and press up against her. Lexi moaned at the pressure and I caught the noise with my mouth. She still had the taste of the chocolate cake we had with lunch on her tongue and I soaked it up, enjoying the way her hips pressed up against me.

"Kaleb," she murmured.

"I know, baby." I rocked my cock against her and let our lips part so that I could pull her shirt and bra off, a little thrill running through me knowing I'd picked these clothes out for her. I tore my own shirt off and pressed her bare skin to mine, relishing the warmth and the way her breast rose in uneven breaths.

"Do you feel the effect I have on your body?" I leaned down, letting my lips trail over her neck till I found the spot that made her whimper and sucked gently. I had to be careful, if I'd left a mark on Lexi right before the wedding, Kat might kill me. I stilled my lips as I waited for Lexi's response and when it didn't come, I thrusted hard against her. "Answer me, baby."

"I feel it. God, it feels good." Satisfied, I resumed kissing her neck, smiling when her hips started to rock against mine. I pulled away and slid her off the counter. She stood, shaking slightly as I pulled away her bottom layers. I kissed my way back up to her lips, then spun her around so that she could see herself in the mirror. Pressed flush against my chest, she looked so small, face flushed, lips slightly swollen from our make out session in the car, and her pussy ... god it was so wet and ready for me.

"See how small you are in my arms, baby?" She nodded, her eyes watching the mirror as my hand slid down her body and to her crotch. I didn't have to go far to feel her wetness, but I pushed two fingers in anyways, stroking her g-spot a few times before pulling out. I held out my hand so she could see her juices stretching between my fingers. "I don't think a kid could make you this wet."

God, I wish I could let this go, but I needed her to ease this insecurity, prove to me that she'd let me take care of her. And she had. I'd spent more money today than any other date I've ever had, she let me delete that jackass's number, but it didn't feel like enough. I wanted to give her the world and I needed to know she'd accept it. Accept me and my love for her.

"No," Lexi answered, the word breathless and her eyes lusted over. I put my fingers to my mouth and watched her moan in the mirror. God that was hot.

"Did you hide some of those condoms in here?" She nodded and pointed to her toiletry bag on the counter. I kissed the top of her head and gave her ass a light tap.

"Get the water started. No telling when anyone will come back and I don't want anyone hearing you. I want those sounds all to myself."

"You're just saying that to sound cool, you really just don't want to get caught," she said, rolling her eyes and smacking my ass as I leaned to grab her bag. By the time I turned back to smile at her, she'd already gotten in the shower. As the water started to run, I shifted through her bag to grab one of the condoms hidden at the bottom.

Stripped down, I stepped into the shower, setting the condom on a shampoo bottle and leaning back to watch as Lexi rinsed her hair, her fingers combing through the long strands. Her hands traveled down along her arms, then up to her breasts, holding them up as she arched her back.

"Are you just gonna watch?" she asked without opening her eyes.

"I thought that's what you wanted me to do." I stepped up and grabbed her by the waist, pulling her into me and relishing the hum of her response. I turned her around and guided her to the wall, her arm bracing against the wall as she rested her forehead there. I leaned into her body, stroking my hard length up her ass. When she moaned, I reached around to her pussy, sticking two fingers inside and thrusting in time with my cock on her ass. My other hand went to her breast, kneading the flesh while my thumb flicked over her nipple.

"Kaleb, please," Lexi whimpered.

"Please what?" I whispered into her ear, my body twitching when she shivered in response.

"Kaleb, don't make me say everything. Women like their men to take action without having to ask." That made me laugh. But if she wanted me to take control, I could do that.

"Is that what I am, Lexi? Your man? Well you certainly use me like I am. Not listening to me when I tell you to slow down, sucking my cock at your leisure despite being out in public, smacking my ass in a room full of kids." With each example, I stroked us harder, her pussy twitching close to relief. "But I like being your man, so it's okay. You can use me however you want or need. The only condition I have is that you come first. And seeing as how most women can't orgasm from penetration alone, I wanna get you a little closer before I get inside you. I want to get you so close, that you'll come on my cock the second it's in. So be a good girl and tell me when you're almost there."

Lexi shivered in my arms, goosebumps spreading despite the warm water falling over us. Her body was burning underneath me and her breaths came in heavy waves. I let my hand fall from her breast, groaning when she whimpered from the loss of my touch, and grabbed the condom, tearing it open with my teeth. I stroked against her ass one final time, before rolling the condom on and positioning it right below where my fingers thrusted into her. She pushed back, squeezing her thighs together, clenching my dick between her legs.

I took her movement as a sign and removed my fingers, ignoring her whimper and taking both hands on her hip and lining myself up.

"I wasn't able to go as fast and as deep as I wanted last night, but I'm going to make up for that now. You ready?" She shook her head eagerly. I kissed her cheek, one last bit of tenderness before I slammed my cock into her. Last night I was too flooded by my own sensation, but now I felt it as she came on me, her walls pulsing and her heat rising. I pulled out so that just my head was inside, giving her one moment to breathe, just one moment, before pulling her hips into me. She cried out my name, the sound shaking through me.

"Kaleb, god, you feel so good," she moaned. The praise made my blood rush and I quickened my thrusts, reveling in the sound of our bodies slapping together.

"Baby, you're the one who feels good. I don't think I could stop thrusting into you if I wanted." I reached around her body to rub her clit, slowly, and brought my other arm around her waist to pin her to me, slowing my thrusts to sharp rocks.

"Be honest, baby, which part of this do you like most? My hand on your clit or my dick inside you?"

"You," she breathed. And fuck, that one word felt like a love confession. I had to choke down the words, not ready to say them out loud for fear of scaring her away. And definitely not wanting to say them while I was slamming into her.

"I need more of you," I said instead. I pulled out and turned her around before she could complain. I reached down and pulled her up by her ass, pinning her back against the wall as she wrapped her legs around me. One small adjustment and I was thrusting inside her again, desperate and needy, and kissing her like she would vanish into thin air.

"Kaleb," she moaned into my lips.

"Yeah, baby? If you come for me one more time, I will too."

"Yes, please come for me, Kay. I'm right there."

Our lips rejoined, tongues caressing and tangling like our bodies. My legs began to tremble as I pushed closer and closer to the edge, but I couldn't have that release until I felt her clench around me again. She just needed one more push.

I leaned down and used one hand to push her breast up so the tip of her nipple reached my lips. I circled my tongue around her before sucking in sharply, her pussy convulsing around me, wringing me for all I'm worth.

When I was finally able to catch my breath, I set Lexi down and rested my forehead on her's.

"How're you feeling, baby?"

"Very good," she breathed. "Though I have to say, if you fuck me like that anytime I so much as accidently imply you're a kid, I might do it on purpose."

"Was that too much?" I said, hiding my nerves behind a laugh.

"No. And I honestly wasn't thinking about you being younger when I wanted to pay. It's just ... you've spent a lot on me the past few days and you don't have a full time job yet and ... I just wanted to pull my share. Feel equal, you know?"

"Aw, I'm sorry, Lex." I took her head in my hands, kissing her forehead and cheeks and nose. "I was pushing my insecurity on you. I'm sorry. Forgive me?"

"Hmm, let me think about it." I kissed her, tongue lining her lips, begging for entrance. When she opened up for me, she moaned at the touch. And when I pulled back she was smiling.

"One condition though," she said, holding up one finger. I kissed it, making her giggle.

"Anything you want, Lex"

"Let me buy things for you. And when we do things together, we take turns paying." I groaned, dropping my head to her shoulder. I knew it was my ego that wanted to be the man and take care of her, but I stubbornly couldn't let go of it.

"Counter offer, I pay for two out of three outings."

"That's gonna be so much harder to track," she said, rolling her eyes.

"That's okay, I'm fine with paying if we can't remember whose turn it is. Good?"

"Fine," she grumbled. I kissed her again, a bubbly feeling filling my heart, those words threatening to slip past my lips again. So to distract myself, I pulled Lex under the water, warming her skin before lathering her up with soap, softly caressing and massaging every inch of her. When she was cleaned and rinsed, I held her against me, leaning against the wall, and said a little prayer that I'd be ready to say those words soon.

CHAPTER 20

Lexi

I sat in the changing room of the church with seven other guys on the morning of Kat and Blake's wedding and I didn't even flinch at the dirty jokes or crude hand gestures. I was too happy to care what those dumbasses were doing or saying. The only bad thing that had happened in the past 24 hours was when Kaleb let go of my hand outside the church. We hadn't needed to talk about it, there was an unspoken understanding that as soon as we said something, our peace, whatever it was that was happening between us, would be destroyed. Plus this was Blake and Kat's day, no need to destroy it by bringing up unnecessary chaos. And I was fine with that. But what I desperately wanted to address, and what I was most afraid to talk about, was what exactly we were doing. I didn't think Kaleb was the type to start something this intensely and not see it through. Especially since he'd argued about paying for our ... dates the way he did. But the thought that this wasn't serious nagged the back of my mind when he wasn't holding me.

"Lex! You got your best man speech ready?" Blake asked when he entered the room, rushing to hug me. Next to me, Kaleb stepped aside to give us space to talk, joining another conversation. I tried to school my expression into a happy smile, but I must've frowned at Kaleb's absence, because Blake asked, "What's wrong? Was Kay picking on you or some shit? You look stiff."

Kaleb looked over his shoulder at us, eyebrow raised and brow furrowed. I wanted to pull him down and kiss away those worry lines. Because I was far from stiff, or at least my body was. After the shower sex and the subsequent actual shower, Kaleb had massaged every inch of my body, insisting that it was the least he could do since we weren't having the most comfortable sex. He had been so serious too, not batting an eye when I tried to goad him into touching more private areas.

"Nothing's wrong, I'm just a little nervous about the speech."

"You don't have anything to worry about. Everybody who matters loves you already."

Instinctively, my eyes met Kaleb's. He was licking his lips, mouth parted like he wanted to say something. This was the first time I'd talk to Blake since Kaleb and I ... started things. And it was much harder to not say anything than I thought it'd be. Especially if Kaleb kept looking at me like that, like he was one second away from sweeping me off my feet and stealing me away.

Shit, Blake knew both of us pretty damn well, it wouldn't take long for him to figure it out. And what would happen then? Because Blake definitely saw his brother as a kid still and he didn't exactly trust my taste in men anymore. He'd throw a fit. Bigger than the time he found out years after the fact that I told Kat she shouldn't date him before they met, even though she assured him that she wouldn't've dated him at the time anyways, because she was convinced she needed to go through a "hoe phase". He didn't talk to me for two weeks.

Maybe if I talked to Kat about it first, she'd help me figure out how to tell Blake. She was already encouraging me to go for it and since it was definitely not just sex, for me at least, I'm sure she'd be thrilled. And with her knowing, that little knot in my chest might start unraveling.

"Okay, boys, time to start getting dressed!" the wedding planner yelled from the other side of the door. I looked back to Blake, who was staring at the door, smiling and rocking back and forth on his feet.

"Excited?" I asked.

"Hell yeah. Man, it's honestly the best feeling, Lex. Better than sex. I can't wait for you to have this too. When we get back from the honeymoon, we'll be your full time wingmen. I for sure owe you for introducing me to Kat. You pick a man out and we'll get him for you. Just as long as it's none of the idiots in this room. I love them, but they couldn't make you happy in the same way Kat makes me happy."

"None of them?" This was a safe test of the waters, right? Because with the way Blake spoke, I couldn't tell if he had ruled out Kaleb or didn't even consider him an option. And that made a difference.

"Nope. Now go get changed. Out the door to the left is a room just for you."

I bit my lip, but nodded and took my suit to the room he mentioned. The room was a closet transformed into a dressing room with sheets covering the cleaning supplies, a bench, and one floor length mirror that was propped against the wall. I could've just changed with the girls if this was what they were gonna do. I got dressed, pulling on each layer and feeling grateful that I didn't have to worry about stepping on my skirt or an odd tan line or sticky bras. I wasn't really sure what I'd done to my tie though, it was lopsided and the knot too big, so I gave up on it and pulled the bench to the mirror to do my hair and make up.

"Lex?" Kaleb's voice called from the other side of the door with a soft knock and my heart rose in my chest.

"Yeah?"

"Can I come in?" I could picture him on the other side of the door, biting his lips, fingers resting on the knob, anxious for permission to enter.

"Yeah, come in." He opened the door so quickly, there was no way I could've braced myself for the image of him. I knew he was going to be in a tux, one the same style as mine, but he wore it well. His broad shoulders filled the fabric, creating hard lines.

My fingers itched to unbutton him, unwrap him like a gift.

"Damn, Lex, you look gorgeous," he said, a lopsided smile spreading across his face. He took hold of my elbows, pulling me to my feet and eyeing me all over. "Where can I kiss you so I don't mess up your makeup?"

I laughed and pulled him into a kiss, running my hands through his hair, knowing he wanted to do the same but wouldn't.

"Where do the boys think you are?"

"Bathroom. Looks like I walked into the wrong room though. Oops."

"Oops," I repeated. Kaleb rested his forehead on mine and started undoing my tie.

"Kaleb?"

"Hmm?"

"What're we gonna tell Blake?" I held my breath, readying myself for a long wait as he thought over his answer, but it turns out I didn't need to, his reply was immediate.

"We don't need to tell him anything."

The response was so quick and it pulled at that nagging thread. We didn't need to tell Blake anything because there was no point to. Kaleb didn't see this lasting, he didn't feel the things I was starting to feel. And that thought broke me. Like being woken up from a beautiful dream by a bucket of ice water.

I reached up to stop his hands, pulling them away before letting go and stepping away from him. He furrowed his brow at me, but waited for me to say something. The problem was I didn't know what to say. I think I'm falling in love with you, but you don't even want to tell your brother, my best friend, about us. I'm falling for you and you have a pattern of not returning those feelings. No, I couldn't say any of that because if I did, I'd be crying all night.

"I've gotta go to the bathroom. You should go back, the guys'll be suspicious if you're gone too long and the ceremony will be starting soon."

"Sure, but are you okay? You look a little pale." He took hold of my hands, rubbing the tops of my fingers as he tilted down to get a better look at my face. The worry in his eyes made me second guess myself. And then I remembered Blake's resounding no to me dating any of his groomsmen. Blake knew me better than Kaleb did, a week of intimacy and sexual tension didn't change that. And I was scared to hear Kaleb confirm what I was thinking. So I chose the easy way out.

"Yeah, I'm fine, it's just the poor lighting and the makeup. I'll adjust it in the bathroom." I practically ran out of the room and I didn't look back. Because I knew if I did, I'd just let myself get dragged around by Kaleb's charming, gentle smile until he got bored of me.

It's fine, I'm fine, I can be strong. It was only a few days, after all. What was there to be upset by? I just had to get through the ceremony, standing next to him, and the reception, where he might ask me to dance. Yeah, it's fine, totally fine.

CHAPTER 21

Kaleb

I fucked up. I don't know what I did or said, but Lexi's mad at me. Everything was going so well too. I hadn't slipped up and told her I loved her. I'd been able to make her happy. We'd gotten through a minor disagreement without me freaking out completely. But now something was wrong.

She was freaked out about something in the changing room. And then during the ceremony, any time I scooted closer so our arms were touching, she stiffened and shifted away. The same thing happened when we were taking group photos. And then when we were seated at the table for the reception, she scooted her chair as close to Blake as possible. And she wouldn't say a word to me. Whenever I asked her a questioned, she'd just hum a response or wave her hands.

At first I thought it was because of her speech, since Blake brought it up in the dressing room. But we practiced it five times yesterday, there's no way she didn't know it by heart. So it had to be something else.

Maybe she thought I was being too obvious and Blake was going to figure us out?

But when she got up to get drinks the second it was appropriate, my anxiety started spiking. Especially when she didn't come back and instead parked herself right on the dancefloor. The only blessing was that she grabbed a bridesmaid to dance with instead of some dude. I watched for a moment, biting my lip as I considered getting up to cut in. But instead, I pulled out my phone.

Me: Sarah, I think I fucked up.

Sarah: Shit, already? Kaleb, when I said your romance was like a romance novel, I didn't actually expect you to have a third act break up.

Me: We didn't break up. Well, I guess we're not actually together. We sort of never talked about that. I mean, it's only been a couple days. I'd scare her if I asked her to be in a full fledged relationship already, right?

Me: Sarah, I'm freaking out. We're at the wedding and she isn't talking to me. She keeps avoiding me and she gets stiff when I stand by her.

Sarah: Okay, okay, calm down. Take a deep breath. What was the last thing that happened before she started acting different?

Me: Um, she was acting a little

nervous ever since we go to the church. But I couldn't exactly be by her side while everyone was around, especially my brother. Then when everyone was changing, I snuck to her dressing room to see her. We kissed and she asked what we were going to tell my brother, I told her we didn't have to tell him anything. He's kind of a dick, I mean I love him, he has his moments, but also, he's my brother, you know? And he literally just told her he wanted her to find love but she shouldn't date any of his groomsmen.

Sarah: Wait, wait, wait. Isn't your brother her best friend?

Me: Yeah.

Sarah: Do you think it's possible she feels bad about lying to her best friend? Or even, she's excited about your relationships and wants to talk about it with him? I mean, I'm not saying your feelings about sharing aren't valid, especially given that it's the dude's wedding day, but still. She probably just needs a sort of deadline or something. Like a concrete "we'll tell him next week" or something.

Me: Fuck, you're right.

Sarah: Damn right I am. Now go

apologize and tell her that you'll tell
your brother soon.

I shoved my phone back into my pocket and scanned the dancefloor to find Lexi with some dude I didn't recognize. She was smiling and twirling her hair, touching his arm. I was up and walking over to her faster than I could think. One second I was sitting down, the next I was by her side, a gentle hand on her elbow. Like hell I was gonna let some stranger swoop and steal her the second I misstepped. I could fix this. I would fix this. And this dude wasn't going to get in the way of that.

"Dude, she's had too much to drink, back off. Lex, let's get you some water." Lexi pulled her arm away sharply and my heart sank.

"Okay, *dude*. What are you? Her boyfriend?" the man asked, laughing at me.

"No, he isn't," Lexi said, looking me dead in the eyes with ... disgust? Hatred? Shit.

"Lex, how much have you had to drink?" I needed to focus on Lex. Mostly because if I gave that dude a modicum of my attention, I'd end up punching him and that sort of aggression would only make things worse with Lexi. And Kat would hate it if I started a fight at her wedding, Blake would probably understand though.

"That's none of your business." She crossed her arms, turning away from me so that her hair swung around.

"Yeah, it's none of your business," the man repeated. I turned to him, stepping close so that he could really comprehend just how much taller I was.

"She's drunk, she's not going home with you. Now leave her alone." The man paled beneath me and made the smart decision to back away. Behind me, Lexi laughed.

"I'm not going home with you either," she huffed. Around us, people were starting to stare and from across the dancefloor, I could see Blake raising an eyebrow at me.

"Let's get you some water and we'll talk, okay?" I moved to her side, wrapping an arm around her shoulders to guide her to the bar. She huffed again but didn't put up a fight. As soon as we were at the bar though, she stepped away from me and her absence felt very cold.

"Can I have that cocktail again?" Lexi asked the bartender, leaning into the counter and giving him a flirtatious smile.

"She's having water." The bartender looked between us, confused.

"No, I'm not. I'll have the cocktail. And there's a …" She shifted through her pocket and pulled out a $20 bill, stuffing it into the tip jar. "A nice tip in it for you."

The man looked at me again and shrugged before fixing Lexi her cocktail.

"Lex, I'm sorry for what I said about Blake. We can tell him whenever you want to. I'll tell him right now if that'll make you happy. Just, please, drink some water and come home with me."

"Tell Blake what? There's nothing to tell him. And I'm not going anywhere with you."

"Nothing?" Fuck that hurt, bad. Did she really have to choose that word? But no, I didn't have the right to be upset. I was the one that fucked up and said shit without considering her feelings, she was just drunk and upset. She probably didn't mean it. God, I hoped she didn't mean it.

"Baby, I'm sorry. I wasn't thinking from your perspective and I said some inconsiderate shit. Please, come home with me and we can talk this out in the morning when you're sober."

"Don't call me baby and quit touching me!" She pulled away from my hand, which had instinctively reached out to her.

"Sir, I think you should leave her alone," the bartender said as he set down Lexi's drink, thankfully with a glass of water.

"I will, I just … Lex, if you're not going home with me, then where're you going?" I took a step further from Lex, my whole body shaking at the wrongness of it. But she obviously wasn't in the right mind to talk. So the only thing left to do was make sure she got through the night safely.

"I'm staying with Rachel." Lex took her drink and stormed off to where Rachel was standing, leaving the water behind. I followed, trying to keep my breathing even, but I was struggling. I thought it was bad when Lexi was mad at me after the strip club, this was so much worse.

"God, Kaleb, leave me alone. You're like an annoying kid," Lexi grumbled when she noticed I followed her. At her side, Rachel gave Lexi an odd look before turning to me and I tried to school my features so it didn't look like I'd just gotten kicked in the gut.

"Lexi says she's staying with you tonight?" I asked and Rachel's brow furrowed.

"Lex, you were serious? She asked me, like, an hour ago, so I didn't think she was serious."

An hour ago, right when the ceremony had ended.

"I'm sorry, are you going back anytime soon she's …"

"Very drunk, I can tell. Blake's normally her guard dog when she's this drunk, but I guess he's busy. And … she doesn't want you to take over?"

"I don't want him to do anything for me ever again," Lexi cut in. My heart was on the floor. No, it was burying itself in the earth, trying to run away from this feeling of dread and despair.

"Hey, Kaleb, do you wanna dance?" someone asked from behind me. I turned to see one of the other bridesmaids, one closer to my age.

"Sorry, I'm not –"

"Go dance with her, Kiddie Kay! I'm sure you were expecting something tonight anyways," Lexi said. Rachel took hold of Lexi, grabbing her by the shoulder and looking her square in the eye.

"Yeah, I'm taking you back to my hotel," she said, linking their arms and moving towards the door.

"But I haven't done my speech," Lexi whined as they went.

"Yeah, you're in no shape for public speaking."

"I'm sorry, I need to make sure they're okay," I said to the woman asking me to dance before running to catch up to them.

"Kaleb, go away, I don't want to see you," Lexi slurred as we stepped into the hallway and away from the party. I took a deep breath and turned to Rachel, because if Lexi said one more word to me I might break down and cry.

"Are you good to drive or do you want me to drive you?"

"Oh, no, I was planning on taking a cab. So we're good on that front, thanks. Plus I don't think Lexi's in a good place to, you know, sit in a car with you."

"Yeah. Um … can I get your number so we can coordinate getting her things? I'll go home now and pack her an overnight bag. Make sure she takes her contacts out before falling asleep. She has a bad habit of forgetting when she's drunk." Rachel nodded, taking my phone when offered and entering her number.

"Just bring everything, Kiddie Kay. I'll leave from the hotel," Lexi said, crossing her arms again.

"Lex, your car is still at my house."

"I'll take a cab and get my car, that way we don't have to see each other."

"Lex, please don't say that. Please? I can't – my parents will be really disappointed if you don't say goodbye." That made her pause, her muscles relaxing just for a second.

"Fine, I'll go say goodbye to them."

"Okay, good. Rachel, I'll text you when I get there."

Rachel nodded and guided drunk Lexi to the door. Lexi looked over her shoulder at me and I stepped forward to say something, but then her face scrunched up and she turned away before I got a chance.

CHAPTER 22

Lexi

"Hey, Lex, you gotta wake up, I have to head to the airport soon."

I grumbled and rolled over in the bed. My eyes opened to an unfamiliar ceiling and I shot up, head swirling around wildly. But rather than the stranger I'd been flirting with at the wedding, I was in Rachel's bed.

"Oh, thank god," I mumbled and reached for my glasses on the bedside table.

"Don't thank god, thank me. And you should probably thank Kaleb while you're at it." Rachel paused her packing, watching me for a reaction. And she got one. My eyes started tearing up and I buried my face in my knees.

"Rachel, do you promise not to tell Blake and Kat?" I murmured, desperately needing someone to talk to about Kaleb. Because when I looked back at him last night, he looked hurt, like I'd just ripped out his heart and stomped on it. If he was just in it for the sex or if it was just a fling, he wouldn't have looked like that, right? And I'd said everything I could think of to hurt them. I wasn't clever, but I was effective.

"God, yes. Though, to be honest, we both know they wouldn't answer the phone right now anyways. But yes, please, I'm dying to know what that was all about." Rachel zipped up her bag and sat next to me, folding her legs to her body and looking up expectantly.

"Kaleb and I were sorta, kinda, hooking up."

"Wait what? Okay, no, define hooking up before I get excited."

"We had sex, a couple times. Once in his treehouse and then in the shower. And I gave him a blowjob in his car in the CVS parking lot."

"Lexi! Oh my god! You got down and dirty with Blake's brother! You little skank, how'd that happen?"

"I don't know. I hadn't seen him in 10 years, he got … he grew up."

"Shut up, we both know he got hot."

"Right, he got hot. And I knew the moment I saw him that I sorta wanted to …"

"Ride that?"

"Rachel, do you want to tell me what happened?

"Sorry, go ahead."

"Okay. So he kept on sorta coming on to me. Like the first party at the Purple Fish, he pinned me to the wall and asked me if I saw him as a man now. And then when I was drunk after the bachelorette party, I asked to kiss him and he told me to ask again when I was sober. And then I got jealous that this striper was giving him attention at the bachelor party and he saw I was mad and wouldn't let it go. And then one of his uncles needed a room, so he gave up his and was gonna sleep on the couch and refused to swap with me or sleep with me because if we were in the same bed together, he wouldn't be able to keep from touching me. And I told him to come to bed with me anyways. And shit, I initiated that more than he did, didn't I?"

"I mean, it sounds like that. But also, Lex, you're a catch. So don't start thinking that he wasn't as equally interested in fucking. I saw how he was looking at you these past few days. Shit, pretty much any time he wasn't talking to someone, he was looking at you. That's why he kept tripping up at rehearsal. Honestly, I should be upset with you, I was the one on his arm getting jerked around. But whatever, why are you guys fighting?"

"We're not fighting, there's nothing to fight about. We never talked about being in a relationship."

"Okay, I'm not buying that. But what was it that made you wanna stop tapping that ass?"

"You heard Kat at the bachelorette. He doesn't date anyone seriously. He's a serial heartbreaker. And Blake told me I shouldn't date any of his groomsmen, probably for that very reason. But for a second I thought he'd be different with me because ... I don't know, maybe because I didn't think he'd risk the awkwardness between me and him and Blake if he was just in it for the sex. But we never talked about it or talked about telling Blake, because ... I was too scared to hear his answer. Then before the wedding

I asked what we were gonna tell Blake. You know I wouldn't be able to keep a secret from him for long. But Kaleb just said we didn't have to tell Blake anything. And he answered so quickly, like he had no intentions of ever telling Blake we hooked up, like it wouldn't last long enough to be worth mentioning. And I couldn't handle that. Not with him. I was already starting to ..."

"Fall in love?" Rachel prompted and I could only nod in response. Rachel pulled me into a hug, patting my back and saying, "I'm only going to bring this up once, because you obviously know him better than me and Blake and Kat had a reason to say what they did. But the way he was making sure you were okay last night didn't seem like the thing a fling would do. Lex, he told me to make sure you took your contacts out. I sure as hell wouldn't have thought to do that. And he packed all your things and brought them here. He missed out on a good chunk of the wedding reception to do that. So are you sure he isn't serious about you?"

"I don't know. I just ... you know I don't have the best track record with men. And I just ..." I cried into her shoulder, clutching her tightly.

"I know, sweetie. I know. Look, I'm not gonna push you to give him a second chance, or even a chance to explain. Protect yourself, trust your instincts. Okay?"

I nodded, not really certain if it was my instincts telling me to run from Kaleb.

CHAPTER 23

Kaleb

L exi Jacobs broke my heart. Or maybe it was more accurate to say I broke my own heart loving her.

She didn't answer any of my texts from last night. Or my calls. And I told myself over and over that she was just asleep, that she was hungover and didn't want to look at her phone. But by the time the morning rolled around, I had no sleep or sense of security that she'd get back to me. Or ever talk to me again. It probably didn't help that I slept on the couch because the thought of being in Blake's bed without her made me want to cry. Damn, that was a fucked up sentence.

> **Me:** Rachel, can you confirm that Lex is okay?
>
> **Rachel:** She's safe, if that's what you're asking. She'll probably be at your house in like 15 - 20 mins to pick up her things/say goodbye to your

parents. You should probably not be there.

Me: She still doesn't want to talk to me?

Rachel: I think you should give her some space, Kaleb.

Okay, so Lexi wanted space, right before she was going home states away from me. Space. She wanted space and I wanted to hold her legs and beg her to stay and take back everything she said last night.

So in order to keep from just waiting by the door and bombarding her the second she drove up, I got ready for a run. Downstairs my parents, Blake, and Kat were talking about the wedding as the newlyweds killed time before their flight.

"What're you doing, Kay? Lex will be here in a few minutes," Blake said once I reached the landing.

"I know, just going for a quick run."

"Really?" Blake got up from the couch and joined me by the door, narrowing his eyes as I put on my running shoes. "Because it looks like you're avoiding Lex. I heard from some of the guys that she was yelling at you last night."

"Well, she was drunk. So, you know."

"Lex isn't a loud drunk. What happened?"

"Nothing, according to her," I scoffed. Maybe it was a good thing that I didn't see her now. She made me feel like a kid last night and not in the unintentional way she had done when trying to pay for lunch. She wanted me to be hurt. And whatever I may have done, it was far from intentional. I don't think I deserved to be in this much pain. Fuck, I was gonna cry again.

Blake didn't seem to like my tone and he moved to block the door and repeated, "What happened?"

"Nothing. Get out of my way. Please."

"Not until you tell me what's going on? Are you the reason my best man didn't give her speech last night?"

"Everything okay, boys?" Kat asked, joining us by the door. Thankfully Mom and Dad were busy packing up all the wedding gifts to mail them back to Blake and Kat's place.

"Kaleb got into it with Lexi and now he's trying to run away from his mess." Blake crossed his arms and shifted his weight so he was standing as tall as possible. Not that it mattered, I had a few inches on him. But that did mean he wasn't going to move.

"Blake, I think you're jumping to conclusions," Kat said.

"She missed the speeches! And she was yelling at him last night. Our Lex doesn't yell when she's drunk."

Yeah, I knew that. Because she was *my* Lex. Or at least she was for a few days.

"I know, but let's be honest, hon, she's not always made smart decisions. She could just as equally be at fault."

No, that didn't sound right. I didn't like the idea of Lexi taking the blame for anything, even yelling at me.

"It's not Lexi's fault. But she doesn't want to see me, so let me go. I'll tell you about it when I get back, once she's gone. Just don't … pressure her to talk about it, okay?"

"She doesn't want to see you?" Kat repeated, her brow furrowing. Blake narrowed his eyes at me, but stepped aside. I didn't give him a chance to change his mind, I strode right out the door and ran.

* * *

I ran for an hour before I came back home. Lexi's car was gone from the driveway and I felt empty. And now I had to deal with whatever bullshit Blake had for me.

I took a deep breath and walked inside. Blake and Kat were waiting for me in the living room, Blake sitting tensely while Kat was strewn across from him. When they saw me come in, Blake's eyes narrowed in on me, but he didn't say anything until I was seated in the armchair across from them.

"Did you guys fuck in my bed?"

"What?" I said, mouth dropping while Kat giggled.

"We have bets going on, Kay, so answer honestly," she said. I couldn't tell if they knew Lexi and I hooked up or if this was a trap to get me to admit it, but what did it matter? I didn't want to tell Blake because he would fuck things up for me and Lexi. But now there wasn't anything left to fuck up.

"No, we did it in the treehouse. And the shower." Kat cheered while Blake hid his head in his hands.

"Thank you, Kay. You've won me the window seat."

"You weren't going to let your wife get the seat she wanted?" I asked, a little shocked given how much of a hardass Blake had been about how I treated Lexi.

"My best friend and my little brother fucked in my childhood treehouse," Blake groaned.

"No, we fucked in *my* treehouse, I helped build it and you never used it," I corrected. Saying it out loud, to Blake, was surprisingly relieving, like a knot in my chest had been undone.

"Blake, honey, I have something to confess," Kat said, a small sheepish smile spreading across her face.

"What? Did you sleep with Lexi too?"

"No, but I did encourage her to have sex with Kaleb."

"Babe!"

"What? I gave her the condition that she couldn't *just* do it for sex. You're a sweet boy, Kay, I know the second you fall for somebody, you're gonna be the best boyfriend ever."

Blake's eyes shot to me narrowing and Kat didn't miss the gesture. Her eyes got wide and she readjusted on the couch so she was sitting on the very edge.

"Kaleb Russel, are you in love with Lexi?"

"He's been in love with her since, like, the second grade," Blake said, crashing back into the couch as his wife squealed.

"It doesn't matter if I love her or not, she doesn't want me for whatever reason. I thought it was because when she asked me about telling Blake I said we didn't have to, cause you'd already told me not to be with her and you're kind of an --"

"Asshole! How could you tell him that? Especially if you knew he was in love!" Kat screamed.

"Because he's never had a serious girlfriend before. You knew that, how could you encourage Lex? She needs someone to build up her security after all those douches."

"But he already loves her!"

"I didn't think he *loved* her, loved her. I thought it was just the remnants of a childhood crush."

"Or he's always loved her, but since Lex was your friend, he thought he never had a chance. So he tried to move on, but he couldn't because he was still hung up on Lexi and that's why all his other relationships failed."

"Am I even a part of this conversation anymore?" I asked, a little concerned how well Kat had me pegged.

"No," Blake said at the same time Kat said, "Of course."

The couple eyed each other for a moment before one of their phones went off. Kat pulled up her phone and frowned.

"Shit, our Uber will be here in a minute. Ok, Kaleb, sum up what went wrong in, like, a sentence or two."

"I really don't know, I tried to call her this morning but she wouldn't answer. And Rachel told me to give her space."

"Does she know you love her?"

"No, we haven't seen each other in 10 years and we only … hooked up a few days ago. I didn't want to scare her off."

"Kaleb! Go tell her now!"

"Now, like call her?"

"Well, no. Go to her apartment. I'll text you her address. Blake, get our bags ready." Blake sighed, but did as Kat asked.

"Isn't it sort of crossing boundaries to just show up at her apartment? I don't want to make her uncomfortable or anything. She said she didn't want to see me."

"That's a very good mindset, but also, you're not crossing any boundaries. You go to her door, tell her you love her, and if she doesn't let you in, you leave. But also, she'd totally gonna let you in."

"How do you know that?"

Kat got up and wrapped her arms around me. "You scared?"

"Yeah."

"You know, when she was here, we didn't bring you up or anything, but she kept looking up to your room. So I think she's a little scared of something too. But love is a little scary."

"That's for damn sure. Do you know how scared I was when you found the jewelry receipt?" Blake said, coming back with two bags under his arm.

"That's not what I was talking about and you know it, dumbass."

"Well, I'm your dumbass."

"Damn right you are." Kat got up, kissing Blake on the cheek before going to the door, carrying the smaller bags. A wave of jealousy crashed through me. I wanted that kind of cute couple shit with Lexi.

"Fix this, bro. Or I'll kick your ass," Blake said,

clapping my shoulder.

"So you're ... okay with this?"

"I'll be honest, it feels awkward as hell. But you're both the kind of dumbasses that would pine for years to come and date shitty people to try and get over one another. That sounds more annoying to deal with than you two actually being together. Just never tell me where you've had sex ever again."

"Deal."

CHAPTER 24

Lexi

I didn't realize how lonely I was, how much I missed Kaleb, until I spent the night in my own bed. Waking up not in his arms, even though I'd only done it twice, felt wrong.

But I couldn't let that bother me. If Kaleb didn't want a serious relationship with me, wanted to avoid saying goodbye to me, then that's his prerogative. Was I hurt that he wasn't there? Yes. Was I secretly hoping he'd force me to tell him why I suddenly pushed him away? Absolutely. But above all else, Kaleb was a respectful man. I said I didn't want to see him, so he stayed away. What else did I expect?

I was surprised that Blake and Kat were there though. And the way Blake was acting, not looking me in the eye, keeping his sentences short, and not giving me shit for missing my speech, I knew he knew something was up. According to Rachel, I'd said some not so friendly things to Kaleb at a relatively loud volume. So there was no way Blake hadn't heard from someone that I was yelling at Kaleb. And he obviously knew I didn't stay with his parents that night. But thankfully he didn't say anything.

What was I gonna do now? I took an extra day off from work so that I could relax, go grocery shopping, do laundry. But now all I wanted to do was watch Tom Hanks' romcoms and cry. And I couldn't even manage to do that. Instead, I laid in bed for hours, scrolling through Kaleb's Instagram in the hopes that I'd see something that proved me wrong. But there wasn't anything new. Kat had tagged him in some of the wedding photos and Jason tagged him in a photo of Kaleb at the strip club getting dragged away by that stripper. But that was it.

When the mindless scrolling started to become exhausting, I meandered to the fridge and bemoaned my lack of ice cream or any other sweets. I probably had the ingredients to make brownies or something, but that would mean dishes. And with my current mood, those dishes would end up sitting in the sink for a week. So delivery it was. Normally I'd go pick something up to save money, but since Kaleb insisted on paying for me so often, I hadn't blown through my wedding budget. Guess that's one good thing to come out of the week.

A knock at the door made me jump and, hand of chest and eyebrows knitted together, I cautiously approached the door. I specifically hadn't ordered things leading up to the wedding so that there wouldn't be any packages just waiting to be stolen at my door, so I knew it wasn't that. But when I took a look through the peephole, I calmed down slightly. I opened the door for the DoorDash guy and he immediately placed a bag in my hands.

"I'm supposed to tell you this is from Kaleb and he's on his way over. And if you still don't want to talk to him, you can just not answer the door," the man read off his phone. When he was done reading, he looked up to me and it took me a second to realize he was waiting for a response. I nodded and the man left. I watched him go, a little dumb founded by what just happened. He had said Kaleb ordered this and that he was on his way, but that didn't make sense. There's no way Kaleb wanted to see me after everything I said to push him away.

I went back inside and unloaded the bag, which was surprisingly heavy. The food was from Hungry Tavern, which I vaguely remember telling Kaleb was my favorite local place. He'd ordered their breakfast special with extra sides of bacon and hash and pancakes, plus two slices of their apple pie. On the receipt, printed under special notes was, "I'd really love to eat this with you if you'll let me. -Kay"

Shit, that made me smile. Had I fucked things up presuming that he didn't want to be serious? Because this screamed, "I'm serious about you." When I dated guys before and started falling for them, they bailed so quick, I was burned. So I started not getting attached or bailing when things started to feel real. Was that what I did to Kaleb?

Another knock came from the door, but this time my heart froze. I tiptoed to the door, looking through the peephole at Kaleb, who stood there with flowers, his eyes closed and his breathing coming out in slow, controlled breaths.

Shit, I had run away. There was no other answer for the way my heart pounded just at the sight of him. I didn't want to get hurt from a fling and I was scared of something bigger.

I cracked open the door, leaving the chain on so that I had one restraint left to protect myself. The second the door creaked, Kaleb's eyes snapped open, immediately finding mine. And he looked ... relieved.

"Oh Lex, god, I was scared you weren't going to open up. Give me just a second, I have a whole thing." He took a few deep breaths and shook out his body. Then he got on his knees, held out the flowers, and said, "Lexi, I still don't understand what I did to scare you and I'm so sorry for that. I wanna know you so well that I can see an insecurity or fear coming up a mile away. I can't do that yet, but if you're willing to teach me, I will. I'll give you all the support and security you need for a lifetime. Because I love you, Lex. And I know that's a lot so soon, but I need you to know because I think not telling you has something to do with how I fucked up. I'm sorry I pressured you to keep things from your best friend. That was selfish of me. You can tell him as much as you want about us, though he did request to not be told about us having sex. And –"

"Kaleb?"

"Yes." He looked up to me with pleading eyes and I knew. Knew in a way I never had before.

"I love you too, Kay."

Kaleb let out a long breath and stood. He reached out to touch my hand through the crack of the door, intertwining our fingers.

"Lex, please open the door so I can kiss you." He let go of my hand so I could close the door and undo the chain. The second I reopened the door, he scooped me into his arms, squeezing hard, the flowers dropping to the floor. Then he let go, hands moving to cup my face, thumbs gently stroking my cheeks. I felt a tear roll down my cheek and he immediately wiped it away. The swell of embarrassment that normally came from crying in front of a guy was immediately squashed by Kaleb's own tears.

And then he kissed me, his touch soft, like he was afraid I'd run away again. God, I'd made him just as scared as I had felt.

"Kaleb, I'm sorry for everything I –"

"How many times?" he interrupted.

"How many times what?" My brow furrowed against his as he rested against me. He looked me in the eyes, his eyes desperate.

"How many times do you want to come tonight? Because making you feel good is all I want to do right now. I wanna prove I'm worth your love, in every way imaginable."

"Kaleb, we should talk first." He licked his lips and nodded. Then he scooped me up and sat on the couch, settling me in his lap and snuggling his head into my shoulder. He squeezed me tight and took one long breath in, making me wish I'd showered today.

"Okay, I'm ready."

"Okay, um, I guess we should talk about what we're doing." It was hard to talk when he was snuggled up on me like this. I could feel both our pulses racing.

"I want to be your boyfriend, partner, lover so bad it hurts. Whatever you want to call it. So long as I get to be with you, I don't care." He started kissing my neck, making me lose track of my thoughts.

"Kaleb."

"Sorry. I was just so scared you were never going to talk to me again," he murmured.

"I'm sorry. I was scared too. I said some things I didn't mean and I know that hurt you. I'm sorry." He squeezed me tighter and I shifted in his lap so that I could kiss his forehead. "So we're ... partners, boyfriend and girlfriend. What about the distance?"

"I've only got two months left of school. You can last two months, right?"

"What about work? You've already got a job lined up."

"Do you really think I'd let a job keep me away from you? I've already got three interviews lined up for places around here. Called around on my drive up."

"You're gonna move here?"

"Of course. Unless that's too much. Is that too much? I'll get my own place, of course. But I don't want to be that far from you."

"But wouldn't that mean you're giving up a good paying job for me? And I'm sure you'll miss your friends in the area."

"Baby, I would give up anything for you, okay? Anything. A job is nothing. Friends? I'll steal Blake's and make them like me better." I laughed and he squeezed me tight again. "And if it makes you feel any better, since I have the offer letter from my current place, I can use that for negotiations. So I won't be losing out on any money."

"And you're sure? Like, one hundred percent certain that you want to do this?"

"As long as you want me by your side, yes. I love you. Fuck, it feels so good to say that out loud."

"It feels good to hear it." I rested my head against him, enjoying his warmth.

"Lex?"

"Mhmm?"

"Are we done talking?"

"Oh, um, wait, no, what about Blake?"

"He knows I love you and he knows I'm here trying to convince you to give me a chance, a real, wholehearted chance."

"And?"

"And he says it'd be more awkward if we were just pining after each other, so we might as well get together. He'll be fine as long as we don't tell him about our sex lives. He was very distraught thinking we'd done it in his bed."

"That's good," I said through a laugh.

"Anything else, love?"

"I think that's all."

"I made a hotel reservation, just in case you – can I cancel it?"

"Absolutely." I shifted in his lap and brought my leg over so that I was facing him, knees on either side of his hip.

"So how many times?"

"I don't know, Kaleb. Did you bring that box of condoms?" The corner of his lip pulled up but before I could see his full smile, he moved in to kiss me, his tongue immediately seeking mine.

"It's in my car, but I'm not particularly inclined to leave you for even a second. Do you have some in here?"

"Yeah, there should be some in the bedside table." Kaleb's lips paused for a moment and he grunted before continuing. "What's wrong?"

"Nothing, love, I just got a little jealous knowing why you have those there."

"Oh." His words weren't the angry blame I've seen called jealousy before, they were soft and grumbled. He was just admitting his feelings, not putting them on me.

"You know what would make me feel better?" His lips moved from mine to my cheek, slowly dipping down to the spot of my neck he knew would make me shiver.

"What's that?" I asked, pushing my hips into him so I could feel the proof of his desire.

"Having you somewhere nobody else has." Kaleb grabbed my ass, his grip firm, and started rocking me against him, making my eyes roll into the back of my head. "Don't keep me in suspense, baby."

"I've only done it on the bed and the couch." I

could barely manage the words. Kaleb's lips left my neck as he looked around my apartment, eyes locking on the kitchen counters.

"Wrap your legs around me, baby," he said as he stood. I wrapped around him tightly, not wanting to leave any space between us and he carried me to the kitchen.

"Kaleb?"

"Mhmm?"

"What do you have against beds?"

"Nothing," he said with a chuckle. "But I want the first time I make you come as my girlfriend to be memorable. Then I'll work on erasing your memories of those other men in your bed."

"I wanna do the same for you," I said as he set me down in front of the counter and knelt down to slide my leggings off, kissing my legs with light brushes of his lips as he went.

"Do what?" he murmured distractedly.

"Erase your memories of other girls." He stopped his kisses and looked up to me with a lopsided smile.

"Baby, you did that the second you kissed me. Now," he said, standing up and taking hold of my waist to set me on the edge of the counter. He nudged my legs apart with his hip and pressed himself against me, holding my face for a forceful kiss. "Let me show you just how much I love you."

Kaleb kissed my forehead then knelt down to the ground. His hands massaged up my thighs, making their way up in slow circles until he reached my center. He spread me open, eyes lusting over before he leaned and licked the length of my sex.

"Fuck, Kaleb. I wanna say I love you, but it feels kind of cheap to say it when you're doing that." I felt Kaleb smile between my legs, then circle his tongue over my entrance before diving in for a taste. He pulled back just enough to look me in the eyes and trailed his fingers over my leg.

"I love you, Lexi." When his fingers reached my center, two circled around and slid inside me slowly, making me gasp. "And I intend to tell you as much as I want, regardless of what we're doing or where we are. And I want you to be comfortable doing the same."

Kaleb leaned back into me, placing soft kisses on my clit, the pressure not lasting nearly long enough. His fingers thrusted slowly, just enough to build up the need inside me, but not enough to release it. He was doing it on purpose, eager for me to say those words to him again.

"Kaleb, you're such a tease," I moaned, feeling a little stubborn.

"And you aren't?" He chuckled, slowing his kisses even more.

"I don't know what you mean."

"The massage in your underwear? Maybe you need a reminder." He slid his fingers out, licking them clean before he started massaging my legs.

"That wasn't teasing, that was enticing."

"I'm enticing you too." His fingers sent chills down my whole body and I gave in.

"God, I love you, Kaleb, but shut up and eat me out." I tangled my fingers in his hair and pulled his mouth forward, cutting off his laugh at my response. He eagerly replied to my request though, raking his tongue over me twice before focusing on the bundle of nerves. His fingers slipped back inside me, curling to press against my g-spot. My fingers clutched his hair tighter and head fell back into the cabinet with a thunk. I felt Kaleb pause and immediately said, "I'm fine, don't stop, please. I'm almost there."

Kaleb gently squeezed my thigh with his free hand and quickened the pace of every point he touched me. The heat twisted and twisted inside me until it all unraveled and shook through me. When my breath slowed back down, Kaleb pulled his fingers away, cleaning them off before licking me clean. He stood and wrapped his arms around me, pulling me so I could wrap my legs around his waist.

"Ready for the bed?" he asked.

"God yes." Kaleb squeezed me tighter to him, letting me feel his hard length against my stomach, and carried me to the bedroom. Once in my room, Kaleb tossed me on the bed, making me giggle until he was on top of me, pinning me down with deep, long kisses. He pulled at my shirt, breaking his kiss only to pull it over my head. Once I was bare for him, his eyes darkened and I heard a low groan sound from the back of his throat. And the sound of his need urged my hands. I slipped my hands under his shirt, dragging the fabric up as I felt his hot skin.

"It's a shame I didn't get to take off your tux," I murmured as I finally pulled his shirt free.

"Yeah? Guess it's a good thing I didn't rent. Do you

want me to wear it next time I come to visit?" I nodded my head eagerly as I pulled down his pants, Kaleb taking over when I couldn't reach.

"When will that be? Actually, first, how long can you stay?"

"I have to leave tomorrow," he sighed, moving to kiss my neck. "But I can come back this weekend if you want. Any weekend you want, just say the word. Then there's Thanksgiving break and then I graduate before Christmas and I'm all yours. How do you want to split the holidays?"

"What?" It was hard to concentrate when he called himself mine.

"The holidays, baby. I want to spend them with you. Each and every one for the rest of my life. So do you wanna do your family one year, my family another? Or do you wanna alternate?" His lips moved down from my neck to my breast, one hand coming up to play with the nipple his mouth didn't occupy. I bemoaned the movement, because now that his pants were off, I wanted to touch him. But Kaleb was too focused on the holiday arrangements to notice my reaching fingers.

"Kaleb, I'm not answering the question until you dick is in my hands."

"Yes, ma'am," he chuckled, arching his back and pulling his hips forward so he didn't have to abandon his fun for me to have mine. "Happy?"

I took him in hand, stroking his full length and rubbing my thumb over his head, enjoying how he shivered in response.

"Yes. We'll go to your family for Thanksgiving and mine for Christmas. I know we just saw them, but Christmas seems more equivalent to a wedding. Happy?"

"I don't think I've ever been happier," he groaned. He rolled over to my side, pulling away from my touch so that he could open up the bedside table. "Oh, you have quite a few toys in here, huh?"

"A few? There's three. That's a perfectly normal number."

"That's a few, did you need to use them a lot?" Kaleb crawled back over me, dragging a pillow with him, which he placed under my hips.

"I mean ... sometimes. When I didn't have anyone or I was on my period or things ended a little ... lackluster." Kaled leaned over to kiss me as he readied the condom.

"Well, you won't need those toys with me, baby. They'll be exactly what toys should be, fun, but ultimately unnecessary. If I'm not satisfying you, you have to tell me. If you're lonely, call me. And I hope it goes without saying that your period is not a deterrent for me giving you what you need." Kaleb pulled up, adjusting himself between my legs and resting his cock at my opening. He eyed me over, a soft smile pulling at the corners of his lips. "God, you're gorgeous, baby. I love you so much."

"I love you too." The words were barely more of a whisper until the final word, which came out in a groan as Kaleb slid inside me. I felt my body stretch for him, be filled by him. And I reached out to pull him closer to me. He obliged with a kiss, one hand moving to pinch my nipple again, driving the need inside me wild. I bucked my hips, crying his name as he reached deeper inside me. Kaleb met my speed, thrusting inside harder.

"God, baby, you feel so good."

"Harder," I whined, making him laugh. But Kaleb took my request seriously, slipping an arm under my hip and angling me so he could thrust in harder for me. That ball of heat started knotting inside me, building more and more pressure with each of Kaleb's thrust, especially when his body came in close enough to graze my clit.

"I'm just about there, baby." I grumbled nonsense, not able to articulate that I needed something else to push me over. "I know, love. I know what it feels like when you're about to come. It only took me once to memorize the feel of you coming on my cock. First, your pussy starts clenching uncontrollably. Yeah, just like that, baby." His words were the push I needed, they guided me into the bursting heat. "And then your breath turns into a pant and your body starts to shiver."

"Kaleb," I cried.

"Yeah, I'm right there with you, baby."

The wave of pleasure crashed over me heavily just as Kaleb moaned into me, his thrust stilling as both our bodies shook. Through heavy breaths, Kaleb covered me with kisses until our bodies cooled and he pulled away to lay at my side.

"God, I'm hungry," I said, making Kaleb laugh

again. He took a few tissues from the bedside table and started cleaning himself.

"Not yet, baby. Two isn't nearly enough. Shame I can't go another round with you myself."

"Kaleb, I am more than satisfied. Let's eat." I sat up and leaned over him to grab tissues for myself, but he took me by the waist and dragged me over his lap.

"I'm not done with you yet. Now, which one is your favorite?" Holding me to his lap, Kaleb leaned into the drawer and shuffled through the completely normal amount of vibrators. I tried to squirm out of his grip, but he held firm. I could probably get out if I really tried, but I wasn't *that* motivated. Though I really was starting to get hungry.

"Just one more, okay? Then food."

"Agreed." Kaleb leaned down and kissed my ass, his scruff tickling and making me squirm some more. "Now, which one?"

"The purple one."

"That was a quick answer."

"It's a vibrator and a clit sucker." I shifted awkwardly, watching as he pulled out the toy and turned it around in his hands. It was kind of hot seeing it against his long fingers, both things for my pleasure. He brought the vibrator up and I shifted so I could watch him slide it in his mouth. He raised an eyebrow at me and I felt heat rise in my cheeks.

"Do you think there are some that have long distance remotes?" he asked, shifting me in his lap so he could reach between my legs and slide the toy in.

"I thought you said they were unnecessary." He

pumped the toy inside me a few times, before lining up the sucker and pressing both buttons at once.

"I also said they were for fun. And I'd like to keep having fun with you when I go back to school."

"And you called me horny," I said, my words somewhere between a laugh and a moan as Kaleb started rocking the toy inside me.

"You are. I know it's too much to ask that you don't drink without, but at least call me afterwards, okay? That way I can talk you through your need. You seem to like that."

I sat up and straddled over Kaleb's lap so I could kiss him. He pushed the buttons again making me melt in his arms.

"I have a feeling I won't be able to get horny after you're done with me," I murmured into his smirk.

"Well, I don't want you to change –"

"Shut up and make me come." Kaleb pressed the buttons three times, rocking the toy inside me as he ducked down to suck my tit. The wave of my orgasm hit hard, my body already so sensitive from Kaleb's earlier handiwork. I dug into Kaleb's shoulders, collapsing into his arms. He rubbed my back softly, before setting me down on the bed. He pulled out the vibrator and set it on some tissues, before grabbing some to clean me up. He was gentle, never putting too much pressure on my overstimulated body. And when he was satisfied with his work, he laid in bed, snuggling up against me.

"What about food?"

"Science shows that couples that snuggle after sex

have longer, happier lives together." His breath tickled the back of my neck, warm and comforting.

"Is that true or are you just making it up because you want to keep me naked?"

"Both."

"You're dumb and I love you, but I'm hungry."

"I love you too, hungry."

God, I was in love with an idiot that told dad jokes. And it didn't scare me one bit any more.

EPILOGUE 1

Kaleb

Lexi has been making me wait for this day for four years. I mean, Lex would say my proposal from four years ago was bogus and didn't count, but still. I'd been eager to marry her from the beginning.

My first proposal came after a few drinks. We were out celebrating my graduation with Blake and Kat right after I moved in with Lex. It was the first time we'd been out with them, minus family events. And while Blake made faces whenever we held hands and told stories about how horrible I was to live with, it was fun. Much better than I expected given how skittish Blake had been at Thanksgiving dinner. And with the excitement and drinks, I slipped up and asked when Lexi would let me marry her.

And she said, "Ask me again when you're sober." So I did. It was the first thing out of my mouth the next morning.

We talked at length about what we wanted in a

wedding, how much it would cost, if we wanted to do couples therapy beforehand, prenups, and what milestones and markers we envisioned as signs of a happy marriage. And after everything we talked about and agreed upon, the only real thing, in my opinion, that we needed to wait on was the money for Lexi's dream wedding. Because like hell I was gonna let her settle for anything less.

So I saved. And saved. And saved some more until I couldn't wait anymore.

Kat somehow managed to get Lexi's Pinterest board without alerting her and then Blake and Kat helped me ring shopping, though to be honest, Blake was absolutely worthless. Apparently Kat had just left magazines around their apartment with the styles she liked circled. But we found the perfect ring nonetheless.

The actual proposal was a mess. I wanted to set up a picnic in my treehouse when we were visiting over the summer. But the candles fell when I was getting Lexi and we came back to a mildly on fire treehouse. No one, or treehouse, was hurt, but it most certainly had me shaking in my boots. But then Lexi laughed. And that laugh was everything I wanted in the world. So I got down on one knee, under the smoldering treehouse, and asked if I could, legally, be by her side forever.

Organs chimed, signaling that the procession was about to begin and my trip down memory lane shut down as I stared at the doors. I shifted on the balls of my feet, excited to see Lex. Blake and Kat came out first, our best man and maid of honor. And then everything started to blur as tears welled in my eyes. Blake stuck his tongue out at me on his approach and Kat pinched him.

When the wedding party lined up at the front of the church, the music shifted and Lexi finally emerged. And damn was she gorgeous. Her dress was all lacey and flowy and hugged her hips. And maybe I should've spent more time watching Say Yes to the Dress with Lex to know what I was talking about, but I was just too wowed to care. She was the most stunning woman to walk the earth.

I still can't believe I'm the one who gets to take that dress off her tonight. And that I get to love her forever.

EPILOGUE 2

Lexi

I rested my head on Kaleb's shoulder, watching Kat make a beautiful and heartfelt maid of honor speech, both of us tearing up a little. Kaleb took hold of my hand, entangling our fingers and bringing it up so he could kiss the back of my hand. The overly expensive engagement ring sparkled back at me. Kat had just finished the story of how she broke into my computer to find my Pinterest list of wedding ideas. I don't think I'll ever have the heart to tell her that she had been bringing up jewelry, rings in particular, a lot, so I got the hint and left my laptop unlocked.

The crowd cheered as Kat finished up and her husband took her place at the microphone. I felt Kaleb stiffen next to me and I moved to kiss his cheek. But then I realized I'd left a lipstick mark, and I got a napkin to clean him up. So I wasn't looking when the crowd gasped. And when I turned to look, Blake was flipping us off. Instinctively, I returned the gesture and a flash went off to the side. Well that will be a great wedding picture. Perfect for over the mantle.

"Now, I know I'm Kaleb's best man and favorite brother." Blake turned back to the audience and continued, "But some of you may remember that at *my* wedding, I didn't get a best man speech. Because these two dumbasses had gotten into a little spat and Lexi got too drunk to give me my speech. So out of fairness, I will not be giving them a speech."

Blake bowed and the crowd booed him as he returned to his seat next to Kaleb.

"Are you happy with yourself?" I asked him, leaning over Kaleb's chest so Blake could hear me over the displeasure of our friends and family.

"I figured it was this or some embarrassing story from when we were kids with a slideshow going on in the background. Honestly, I prefer this," Kaleb murmured, pulling me up for a soft kiss. God, I couldn't be mad, not today, not when I'd just married the love of my life.

"Don't worry, I still did the slideshow," Blake said, and right on cue, the projector in the corner of the room lit up with photos of us as kids. Every few photos, Blake had scribbled some notes on them. A picture of Blake and me at the beach had a scribble separating us and a scribbled note that said, "I found this half of the photo under Kay's pillow when he was 13."

"Wait, really?" I pulled away from Kaleb so I could see his face and it was so red.

"Blake, what have I ever done to you that made you feel this was necessary?" Kaleb asked, covering his eyes with his hand. I pulled his arm away and kissed him.

"I think it's sweet. Though honestly, not the best photo you could've used."

"I didn't use it for anything," he grumbled.

"No one's buying that, bro," Blake said.

"Bro? Sorry, I don't have a brother. Only a lovely sister who gave the most heartwarming speech at my wedding. I love her dearly."

"Aw, thanks, Kay, I love you too," Kat said, though she had been snapping photos of Kaleb's embarrassed reaction. Then the slideshow shifted to pictures from my college days and Kaleb's high school days. Then there was Blake and Kat's wedding with notes about how obvious it was that we'd been arguing. And then there was our engagement photo, Kaleb on his knee, the treehouse not looking like it was just on fire. But the beautiful picture was ruined by the note. "This is where they first went at it. And if I have to live with that knowledge, you do too."

"Blake, our parents are here," Kaleb said, jerking to face his brother.

"Babe, don't kill him here. There are witnesses," I said through a laugh.

"Can you wait to kill him until, like, a month after I raise his health insurance. If I'm going to be a widow, I wanna be a rich one," Kat said. Kaleb settled back into his seat and nodded. I took his hand and brought it to my lips, the memory of our first time together making me a little restless for our wedding night. Kaleb had insisted that we not sleep together last night, because he said things were always more intense when we'd been apart for a bit, but I knew he was just trying to be romantic. I tried to talk him out of it, had sent him several pictures to entice him to come back to my room and complained about how cold the bed was without him. But he held firm.

"Whatcha thinking about?" Kaleb asked, leaning into me.

"How much I love you."

"Hm, I think that's bullshit. But me too."

"'You too' as in you love me too or you're thinking about what I'm thinking about?"

"Both." He leaned in to kiss me again. And I smile because I get to kiss these lips for the rest of my life.

ABOUT THE AUTHOR

K.E. Monteith is an adult romance writer living in Northern Virginia, with her two rambunctious dogs and partner. Her debut novella, ALL GROWN UP, is a gender-swapped brother's best friend romance released in February 2022. And her upcoming novella, QUITTING MY BOSS, is an office romance coming out in December 2022.

BOOKS BY THIS AUTHOR

Third Time's The Charm

LUCY SHEPPARD

Ten years ago Jake kissed me and ran. Eight years ago I learned the reason why. Five years ago, Jake came back for a night and I let him have what we both wanted, knowing he wouldn't be able to stay in town after all he went through.

But that night led to a kid. And while I wouldn't take it back for the world, now that Jake's made a surprise visit and finds out he's a dad, I can't let my love for him sway me anymore.

JAKE WHEATLEY

Ten years ago I stole Lucy's first kiss because I thought it'd be the only thing I could have from her. Five years ago I took something even more important. And now I found out that night led to a kid. Lucy and my kid.

I can't be a father, not when mine was the way he was. But I can't bring myself to leave Lucy's side this time. Maybe if it's just a little, I won't turn out like him.

Third Time's the Charm is a standalone, steamy romance. This novella does contain material triggering for some: sexually explicit content, depictions of parental abuse, neglect, and demotic violence, and a depiction of panic attacks.

One Dropped Key

Kasey doesn't regret letting Matt stay with her while he's been in-between places. But she is getting frustrated. Frustrated with his shoes in the doorway. Frustrated with her lack of alone time. And very frustrated by his gorgeous arms.

So when Matt steps out of the house and she has a few minutes alone, she takes some more "drastic" measures to make sure she's taken care of before he gets back. But when she accidentally drops the key and needs Matt's help, he's not sure she's done being cared for.

ONE DROPPED KEY is a steamy, short, roommates to lovers romance with a mildly ridiculous setup. There are sexually explicit scenes, including minor bondage and praise kinks, and a happily ever after.

Quitting My Boss

Morgan Bleckard and Rachel Conrad have the perfect boss-to-assistant relationship. There are good benefits, plenty of PTO, decent health care, and copious amounts of sex with the boss.

But as Rachel approaches 30 and feels pressured to settle down, she decides to quit her job, and her boss, to become exclusive with another guy. But Morgan never saw their relationship as just sex. And he'll do anything to get her back, to have her as his, for real this time.

QUITTING MY BOSS is a steamy workplace romance between boss and assistant, featuring dual POV, flashbacks to heated moments, and a HEA. This book features sexually explicit scenes that are not appropriate for those under 18.

UPCOMING RELEASE

CONTINUE READING FOR A PREVIEW OF

Quitting my Boss

K.E. MONTEITH

PREVIEW OF
QUITTING MY BOSS

Morgan Bleckard, CEO of the largest chain bookstore in the Northeast, the hottest bachelor in the city, had the hots for me. Which was admittedly an egotistical thing to say given the fact that I'd only been working for him for a month. As his secretary. I mean, come on, The rich beyond belief boss having a thing for his secretary? That was too stereotypical, too book-trope-y to be real. Except …

"Rachel." I turned in my chair to face the man of all my recent hot dreams. He leaned against the doorframe to his office, sharp lines of his navy suit shifting as he crossed his legs. Mr. Bleckard didn't say anything for a long moment, leaving me no other choice than to stare at his full lips in anticipation. No one would blame me for thinking about how those lips would feel on my skin. Especially when I finally met his eyes and the light green I was becoming used to were overshadowed by hunger.

Mr. Bleckard's eyes trailed down my body slowly, making goosebumps bloom. The man gave me goosebumps every damn time he looked at me like that. And he did it a lot. The other day, after I handed him the weekly manager reports, he'd tossed a crumbled sheet of paper towards the trash can. Towards. Not in, but right in front of. And then he asked me to pick it up on my way out. I could feel his eyes on my ass the whole time and it gave me a sort of ego trip. Especially when he made some sort of guttural noise when I bent over. I dreamed about that noise all the time now.

Thinking of those dreams Bleckard inspired had me shifting in my chair and I crossed my legs, like that could keep the need pinned in place. But the action drew his gaze to my thighs, where my pencil skirt had ridden up slightly. Bleckard's throat bobbed before he shook his head and returned to his office.

I don't know what compelled me to get up, probably lust if I'm being honest, but I did. I followed him into his office and stopped a few feet inside. "Did you need something, sir?"

Bleckard turned to face me and sighed. He paced the length of his glass desk, just one of the many modern pieces of furniture in his office I pictured him taking on. The cold glass would make for a nice contrast to the heat of our bodies.

I bit my tongue and tried to drag myself away from the fantasies by looking around. There wasn't much in his office to distract me. No pictures, no decorations, no cup of colorful pens. The man was all business, all of the time.

Finally, Bleckard stopped his pacing and faced me, leaning against his desk. "Do you feel like you can say no to me?"

The question caught me off guard. The words were delivered flatly but his hands were gripping the desk so tightly they were turning white. And the same thing that compelled me to come into his office moved me to speak.

"Yes, sir. I can tell you no."

Bleckard pushed himself up and took long steps towards me. Then he reached me and kept going, I stumbled back until my ass hit the door, slamming it closed. One of Bleckard's hands braced against the door, the other taking my chin and tugging so I met his eyes.

"I *need* you, Rachel. *Badly*. Yes?" Mr. Bleckard tilted his face down, his heavy breathing ticking my cheek.

"Yes." I don't know how I managed the word with his lips right there. He sucked a breath in, teeth sinking into his lips. Bleckard dropped his hand from my chin, grazing his fingertips down from my shoulder to my waist, which he grasped firmly. He pulled my hips to his and I gasped. Partly because of the sudden and bold move, but mostly because I was now pressed up against the hard bulge in his pants. A hardness that made my mouth water.

"Is there anything on the calendar today?"

I couldn't for the life of me remember a single thing that was on the calendar. But I could remember Bleckard explaining that he didn't take meetings on Tuesdays because Mondays were for fixing problems that happened over the weekend and Tuesdays were to catch up. Something about the logic stuck with me.

"No, sir." As soon as the words were out of my mouth, Morgan's lips were on me. He didn't start with my mouth though, he started with my neck. Open mouth presses against my skin, sloppy and hungry.

For a second, the thought of Morgan being my boss and this being a bad idea crossed my mind. But what was the worst thing that could happen from a fling with my boss? Getting fired? I'd survive that. If how turned on I was right now was any indication, sex with Morgan would be worth it.

As Morgan's lips trailed their way up my neck, I fisted my hands in his jacket and pulled him closer to me. The fabric was so smooth, cool to the touch, and God, I wanted more already. I shifted my weight to push against the door and wrapped a leg around his waist, keeping him pinned against me while I worked his buttons.

Morgan smiled into my skin before sucking at my neck and drawing a groan from somewhere deep inside me, somewhere that hadn't been touched like this, ever. But it felt like too much too soon. Instinctively, I stopped undressing him and put a hand over my mouth to stop the sounds of eagerness leaking out of me. Morgan pulled back, taking his hand off the door to grab my wrist and pull my hand away.

"This office is soundproof. No one will hear you but me." Morgan's hands moved to my waist, pulling me up to wrap my other leg around me, using his hips to pin me against the door. "And I want to hear every sound you make. Don't hold anything back from me."

Oh, so that's how it was. Morgan didn't talk much. He spoke in simple, direct sentences. Apparently, he was saving his talking energy for this. For saying things that made my cunt pulsate and hips rock into him. And apparently, that action had a similar effect on Morgan as his words for me, because he let out a sound that vibrated through his whole body.

Then he took my mouth. And when I say took, I really mean it. One hand went into my hair, tangling and gripping tightly before tilting my head and bringing our lips together. He wasn't soft or slow, but all-encompassing and hungry. His lips, just as soft as I'd imagined them, parted and his tongue glazed over me. The move made me moan, parting my lips and letting him lick into my mouth. The feel of our tongues meeting was hot and twisting. Morgan's hand that remained on my waist slid down my thigh and back up my skirt to grip my ass. His hold was tight, gripping me with all the need I felt.

"These skirts have been driving me insane." Duly noted. That was the perfect excuse to buy every color and pattern available. His hand slipped under my panties, messaging my ass and rocking me into him. Yes, I'll definitely buy those skirts. But then, just as my eyes rolled to the back of my head, he mumbled, "Don't wear them on Mondays. I need to get work done, for fucks sake."

Huh. Guess I don't need to buy more skirts after all. Bummer. But reasonable, I guess. We were technically supposed to be working.

Morgan let go of my hair and started working

my buttons down and my hands moved to do the same. Our wrists clashed, desperation making our movements sloppy and slow. When the frustration reached its boiling point, buttons went flying. Morgan stared down at my chest for a moment, nostrils flaring. I didn't think he noticed that I'd also torn open his shirt, until he leaned down to my breast, his lips brushing my skin, and murmured, "Put the shirts on my card."

"Yes, Morgan." The words came out breathy as his hands wrapped around my bare waist and made their way up to my breasts. But he stopped when I'd said his name, fingertips just under my bra. His eyes had gone wide, the lust dulled by something else. Shock, maybe. Was I in the wrong to say his name? I mean, we were about to fuck and even if this wasn't something serious, saying his name shouldn't be a problem. Or did using his name reminded him of our position? Reminded him that he was my boss and he shouldn't be fucking an employee, even one who was eagerly giving her consent.

"You can't do that, Rachel. It's too much." His hands slid further up, pinching my nipples and drawing out a sharp groan. "Understand?"

"Yes, sir." That shouldn't have been my answer. I should've stopped right there. If a man wasn't gonna let me scream his name during sex, then I shouldn't be fucking him. But I wanted Bleckard so badly. And it's not like I was looking for something serious anyways.

Bleckard abandoned my breast, undoing his buckle and zipper and pulling out his thick and impressively hard cock. Drool pooled under my tongue as rubbed against me. His hands returned to my thighs, running up until his fingers reached my panties, pushing them aside and sliding a finger over my clit. His cock twitched against my leg as he slid his finger into my pussy, curling until I screamed for him.

"So fucking wet for me."

"Yes, sir." And from there on I was a fucking goner.

Made in the USA
Middletown, DE
04 September 2022

73167839R00129